ALI SPARKES

MONSTER MAKERS

Electrotaur and Slashermite

To Jacob and Alex, creators of Taurs

First published in the UK in 2008 by Scholastic Children's Books
An imprint of Scholastic Ltd
Euston House, 24 Eversholt Street
London, NW1 1DB, UK
Registered office: Westfield Road, Southam, Warwickshire, CV47 0RA
SCHOLASTIC and associated logos are trademarks and or
registered trademarks of Scholastic Inc.

Text copyright © Ali Sparkes, 2008
Illustration copyright © Dynamo Limited, 2008

The right of Ali Sparkes and Dynamo Limited to be identified as the author
and illustrator of this work has been asserted by them.

Cover illustration © Steve Sims, 2008

ISBN 978 1 407 10291 7

A CIP catalogue record for this book
is available from the British Library

Printed by
CPI Bookmarque, Croydon, CR0 4TD
Papers used by Scholastic Children's Books are made from wood grown in sustainable forests.

3 5 7 9 10 8 6 4 2

This is a work of fiction. Names, characters, places, incidents
and dialogues are products of the author's imagination or are used fictitiously. Any resemblance to
actual people, living or dead, events or locales
is entirely coincidental.

www.scholastic.co.uk/zone

Chapter One

Runny Mead

"There's going to be death," warned Lewis. "Lots of really messy death with this one. His arms are like skewers, you know ... like twisty things that skewer your head and he's mean. He'll skewer you dead. Deader than anything."

Jack screamed.

Sarcastically.

"Skewers? He sounds like a barbecue monster to me. Has he got a stripy apron on?"

Lewis glared at him and made vicious darting movements with his pencil – but he glanced down at his monster's curly, pointy arms, reaching wonkily across the bit of white paper, and a worried frown wove across his face. He picked up a red crayon and began putting gory drips of red on the end of them, to be on the safe side.

1

Jack snorted. "If you want scary, take a look at Krushataur!" He held up his piece of paper, upon which a beast of unimaginable horror crouched, drawn in thick black felt-tip with yellow hazard stripes along its boxy body. Its eyes were red and swirly and its arms were like great big jagged pincers.

Lewis peered at Krushataur. "What's that in its claw thing?"

"It's a *human head!*"

Lewis raised one eyebrow, "It looks like a baked bean."

Jack huffed. "It does *not*! Krushataur is way scarier than Skewertaur. I wouldn't even let Skewertaur into Tauronia. He'd wet his pants."

The doorbell rang as Lewis opened his mouth to argue. Mum went to answer it and there was a bright chuckle in the hall. Aunt Thea was here. Lewis seized his picture of Skewertaur

and ran to hug his favourite aunt. Jack followed quickly, carrying Krushataur.

Aunt Thea looked fabulously out of place in the neat beige hallway. She was dressed from head to toe in turquoise silk, with a black lace scarf at her throat and scarlet leather boots, with buttons done up at the front and sharp points at the toes. Her long dark red hair hung in a shining plait down one shoulder.

"Lewis! Jack! How lovely to see you!" She held two packages of crumpled green tissue paper in each hand which biffed against them as she gave both boys an enthusiastic squeeze. "What have you been making to go into Tauronia?"

Jack and Lewis proudly showed Aunt Thea the latest Taurs. She knew all about Tauronia and seemed endlessly fascinated by the creatures her nephews drew to live there. Tauronia was the land of the Taurs which they'd made up. About twenty-five Taurs now lived in this huge, storm-swept, violent land, in caves or volcanoes or castles or towers or broken ancient flying machines. Some were pure evil. Some were just bad-tempered and a few were quite nice, even though they usually looked terrifying.

"Eeugh!" gasped Aunt Thea, looking at Krushataur. "He looks nasty. Is that a. . .?"

3

"Human head. Yes," said Jack.

Aunt Thea shuddered dramatically and then picked up Lewis's.

"Skewertaur!" marvelled Aunt Thea. "I wouldn't like to get on the wrong side of him! What would he do?"

"Skewer your eyeballs out, probably," said Lewis.

"That would be unpleasant," nodded Aunt Thea. "Has he got a quest yet?"

Lewis considered. There always had to be a quest.

"I think. . ." he said, at length. "He's going to seek out the Sapphire Sphere of Density."

Aunt Thea nodded. "The Sapphire Sphere of Density *should* be found," she agreed.

"*Destiny* – not density, you noob," said Jack. Lewis pulled a face at him.

"How about the Fantastic Flickering Fork of Fate?" asked Aunt Thea. "You never did tell me what happened about that."

"It's back in the Cataclysmic Cutlery Drawer of the Kitchen!" cut in Mum. "Where it belongs! Shall we put the kettle on?"

They went back down the hall into the kitchen, and Jack and Lewis settled themselves happily back at the table as Mum and Aunt Thea began talking and making tea. The crumpled green packages had

been placed on the draining board. Jack and Lewis knew they just had to wait.

At Easter, Aunt Thea, just returned from Russia, had brought tiny green eggs made into fantastic little boxes on dainty silver legs. They had a hinge and you could flip back the top to see the curved inside, painted gold and varnished hard.

Just before last Christmas, after a trip to Peru, Aunt Thea had returned with an armadillo curled up into a weird basket, with its tail touching its little dead snout, making a handle, lined with velvet along where its insides must've been. "It's strictly illegal of course," she'd told them. "But it's an antique – made forty or fifty years ago. You couldn't get one today."

Ostrich feathers, porcupine quills, ancient gods carved in soapstone, Indian dream-catchers made with tanned buffalo hide, old wooden Chinese puzzles that clicked and clacked, a jade monkey which climbed up and down a glass ladder, strange-smelling plastic gel that made coloured bubbles which set hard like glass, and a heavy, knotty wooden stick, which, when you turned it up on its end, made a noise like a shower of rain in a forest. All these wonderful things came from Aunt Thea. She *never* gave them children's things. What's

more, she never, *ever* told them to be careful or not to break them.

After a few minutes of tea and chat Aunt Thea said "Oh! I almost forgot!" There was a merry glint in her eye. She knew full well that her nephews had been squirming with excitement over the packages on the side. "Look what I brought you from the valleys!" She handed them both a package and in a couple of seconds they were each holding up a strange thing.

Jack fished his glasses out of his pocket. Sliding them on to his nose, he peered at what looked like a piece of tree and felt its rough, knotty texture in his hands. It was about as tall and wide as a medicine bottle – in fact – they *were* bottles. The chunks of branch were roughly carved into little containers, even with bits of stubby twig still on them. The base of each wooden flask was flat, so they would stand upright, and the necks were round and narrow, with a small cork jammed into them.

Jack and Lewis marvelled at them. Jack eased out the small cork and heard a "tuk" noise. He peered inside and saw nothing but an inky darkness and a glitter of light reflected in it. He gently shook the bottle and it slooshed delicately.

"What's in it?" he asked, and sniffed the bottle. It

smelled rich and warm and sweet – like raisins and mint and honey mixed up with something stronger.

"Merrion's Mead!" said Aunt Thea, with great satisfaction.

"Mead?" said their mum. "But that's alcohol! Oh Thea!"

"We won't drink it!" said Lewis. "But what *is* it for?" asked Lewis. He'd uncorked his and was squinting with one eye, trying to see inside.

His aunt leaned over to him, and her turquoise beads slid and skittered across her shoulders like an excited snake. "I'm not sure I should tell you this," she said, narrowing her eyes. "It could be *dangerous. . .*"

Chapter Two

Spills and Thrills

"I found these bottles in the darkest corner of a very old shop in a small Welsh village, at the foot of a mountain upon which stands a medieval castle," said Aunt Thea. "The man who sold them to me said that the lord who lived in the castle, many centuries ago, once asked every wise woman in the village to create the perfect drink to fill his prized goblet, which was made of Welsh gold and set with rubies. The drink had to be perfectly sweet and perfectly wet, perfectly cool on the tongue and perfectly hot in the throat. Only one wise woman could do this, and rumour has it that this woman was a witch – because not only was the drink the most delectable flavour and most fabulous feeling in the world – it also had the power to bring the stuff of dreams . . . *alive!*"

Aunt Thea stared at them both, her brown eyes sparkling like her beads.

"Is that true?" asked Jack. He really *wanted* it to be true – but he was nine now, and felt he should check.

"The drink," went on Aunt Thea, "was called Merrion's Mead – after Lord Merrion, who had asked for it. Sadly, the lord forgot that as well as good dreams, we all have *bad* dreams too. He'd had night after night of dancing with princesses, flying with unicorns and turning his trees into barley sugar and eating them – but after drinking three cups of mead late one evening, he had a nightmare and was chased into his own moat by a giant pillow, and sadly drowned."

There was a moment's silence. Lewis looked horrified but Jack was pursing his lips.

"How did anyone ever *know* that he'd been dreaming about being chased by a giant pillow?" demanded Jack, and Aunt Thea threw back her head, clapped her hands and laughed.

"That's just what I said!" she beamed. "Now – get on with your Taurs, boys. Your mum and I have grown-up stuff to talk about."

Jack and Lewis examined their gifts for a few minutes, then they put the corks back in and placed the bottles on the table next to their drawings. Jack went back to drawing

ELECTROTAUR and Lewis screwed up the last picture (he had a habit of going off his creations) and started a fresh one of SLASHERMITE.

Electrotaur was a tall, golden scaly creature, standing up like a man, but with a spiky tail, the head of a dragon and claws like bits of lightning. Jack frowned at the criss-cross yellow and red pattern he'd just drawn on Electrotaur's legs. It was meant to look like fire, but was more like the trousers his grandad wore on the golf course. He wasn't sure that this really *worked* on a terrifying electrical monster.

Lewis was doing better with Slashermite. His Taur's little purple head had spiky ears and a horn in the middle, like a rhinoceros. The rest of his body was covered in purple crayon zigzags. His claws were sharp; used for slashing – but actually, Slashermite was only a baby, said Lewis, and though he looked scary, was really a goodie.

"Electrotaur's not really bad either," said Jack, putting an electrical glow and a few sparks at the

end of his creation's tail. "Well – sometimes he is. He *can* be really mean. But not if you give him doughnuts. Doughnuts always turn him good."

Jack went on about Electrotaur a bit more while he tried to improve the trousers, but Lewis was engrossed with Slashermite, who was coming along nicely. Scrag the cat pushed the kitchen door open, and Mum and Aunt Thea's voices could be heard from the dining room. Aunt Thea sounded serious now. "He's managed to get everyone else to sell," she sighed, "and to be honest I probably would have too by now. But he won't protect the standing stone, I know it. So I can't move."

"Oh, Thea," sighed their mum, "it's only a chunk of rock! You can't let a chunk of rock rule your life."

"Cara, that standing stone is important to the world," said Aunt Thea. "You never did understand about these things." Jack bit his lip.

He knew Aunt Thea was right. Mum didn't have much imagination. The fantastic bit of rock that stood up like a giant, slightly crooked finger in Aunt Thea's back garden was rumoured to date back to the Stone Age. But it wasn't officially protected like other standing stones might be, so Aunty had always felt she must protect it herself. She liked to dance around it at dawn on the summer solstice, and sometimes had a few friends around to join in.

He and Lewis had long ago decided that the stone was a special Taur stone marking the way to their fabulous made up-world of Tauronia. Tauronia was their favourite game and always best played in Aunt Thea's garden. You had to run around and around the standing stone until you went dizzy and fell over. It was when you were lying on your back and the sky was spinning above you that you could sink down into Tauronia, said Lewis. Not that this was necessarily a good idea. You might drop right on to Grippakillataur's head and be squished in his mouth, which was like a giant car crusher, with a green tongue. Or maybe you'd stumble into Lavataur, who dripped across the landscape, a smoking, oozing lump of molten rock with blue

eyes. He could give you a nasty burn, although he wasn't really that bad. Lavataur liked to have his back scratched with a fork, but it was hot work and you could lose your eyebrows.

Most Taurs were scary and dangerous – although not necessarily bad. Many were monster heroes. Terrifying to look at but brave and mighty. The Mites could be dangerous too, but they were smaller and were generally easier to play with and their quests were more fun and less likely to end in slaughter. Lewis first thought up the Mites. Aquamite was a good laugh. He was amphibious and scaly, with slightly goofy orange teeth, but if you were nice to him he'd let you go underwater in a giant bubble with him and bob around in the hot jets from the volcanoes, watching the weird Tauronian fish.

Jack sat back, looking at his picture. It was finished. Lewis's was nearly done, too, although there was still half of Slashermite's tail to be drawn. Lewis was now babbling happily about Slashermite's habits – some of which sounded fairly disgusting.

"Lewis – why have you always got to be so revolting?" said Jack. "Don't make him eat out of the toilet!"

"He's my Taur! He'll eat what *I* say!"

Jack decided to ignore Lewis. He lifted his picture.

"I give you..." proclaimed Jack. "Electrotaur!" He made a grand sweeping gesture with his arm, and promptly knocked over both of the curious wooden bottles. They landed with such a sudden crack that both corks popped out – and in moments a small, pale yellow river of Merrion's Mead was flowing across the paper they'd been drawing on.

"JACK!" yelled Lewis, furiously grabbing up his mead bottle and his picture in each hand.

"Sorry!" said Jack, righting his bottle too. "Oh no! It's nearly all spilled out!"

Dismally, they both shook their bottles, and discovered that only a tiny bit of Merrion's Mead was still in them. The rest had meandered across the table top and seeped into Jack's drawing. More was dripping off the edge of Lewis's artwork, as he glared at his brother.

Jack grabbed the nearest cloth and began to mop up the mess. It smelled wonderful, but didn't look too good. "Oh no – it's done for Electrotaur!" he groaned, but then he picked up his picture and looked at it thoughtfully. The mead had blurred his creature's scaly face a little – but at the same time, it looked quite good. Strange.

14

"Boys – bedtime! Up you go now," called Mum from the front room.

"We'll put them on the radiator in our room," said Lewis. "They'll dry off in no time. Shame about the mead. It's nearly all gone!"

The sweet meady scent drifted around their bedroom as soon as the paper creatures were laid on the top of the radiator. It sent them off to sleep fast.

When Jack next opened his eyes it was the middle of the night and very quiet. What had woken him up? It had felt as if a sudden draft had rushed across his face. And there was a strange glow in the room. Jack sat up in bed, his mouth fell open, and he stared and stared.

Standing by the radiator, eight foot tall and buzzing with a strange blue light, stood Electrotaur.

Chapter Three

Undone Tails and Dreadful Trousers

Jack slid to the edge of the bed and, never taking his eyes off Electrotaur, kicked his feet down towards Lewis's head, hoping to wake him. A muffled, sleepy protest confirmed that he'd hit the target.

"Lewis! Lew!" hissed Jack, his heart thundering in his chest. "Wake up!" Electrotaur turned his scaly head towards his creator and sparks of blue electricity danced in his green eyes.

Lewis *had* woken up. "Jack..." his voice wobbled. "There's something on my bed." There was a tearing sound.

Jack swung his head upside down to peer under the bunk. Sitting halfway up the quilt, roughly the same size as his little brother, and with a rhino horn in the middle of his purple forehead, was Slashermite. The tearing sound

16

Jack had heard was the creature's razor-sharp claws, which were running up and down Lewis's duvet cover. In the blue glow from Electrotaur, little fluffy bits of duvet filling were starting to waft about and Slashermite's face could be clearly seen. The look on it was not fierce or menacing, but curious and distracted, like a boy working out a new computer game.

Lewis sat up. "If you keep doing that," he said, switching on his bedside lamp, "we're going to be in a lot of trouble with my mum!"

Jack froze, hanging upside down, his mouth a round "O" of alarm. He waited for Slashermite to gore Lewis with his rhino horn, or slash him with his terrifying hands.

But Slashermite just looked embarrassed.

"Oh – sorry," he said, in a voice remarkably like Lewis's. "It's just that they're all new and shiny, and I feel like I just *have* to *do* something with them."

"Well – just – don't do something on my *bed*!" said Lewis.

"OK," said Slashermite, and meekly folded his knife-like talons into his palms.

Jack was just about to ask Lewis if they were actually *awake* when his feet lost their anchor at the far side of the mattress and he fell head first on to the bedroom floor. The whack on his skull convinced him that he wasn't dreaming.

"You all right?" asked Lewis.

Jack stared from Lewis to Slashermite to Electrotaur, who was still humming and motionless by the radiator, one lightning-fingered hand holding on to it and making the whole thing hum along with him.

"All right?! All right?!" he squawked. "There are two monsters in our bedroom! Of *course* I'm not all right!"

"It's OK," said Lewis. "They're not baddies. They're goodies. That's how we made them. Right?" he looked towards Slashermite for agreement and his creation nodded and smiled, slightly sarcastically, revealing a set of very white teeth in a pair of very red gums.

"Yes. This is how you made *me*," he said. He didn't sound very pleased; like their father when he looked in the mirror after Christmas.

"What's wrong with how I made you?" asked Lewis. "*I* think you're brilliant!" Slashermite slipped off Lewis's bed and stood on his clawed feet, accidentally marking two sets of grooves into the carpet. He reached behind himself, picked up a long purple spiky thing with a lopsided, frayed end, and waved it once at Lewis.

18

"Oh!" Lewis bit his lip. "I didn't finish your tail, did I?"

"Ha!" cackled Jack, feeling a lot less scared now. "You gave him half a tail!"

A blast of prickly heat struck him on the back of the neck and he spun round with a gulp. Electrotaur was giving him a hard stare.

"AND YOU? YOU MAY LAUGH?" he said, in a metallic kind of voice. He pointed to his trousers, which were just as dreadful in three dimensions as they had been on paper. They were red-and-yellow checked.

Lewis started giggling. "He looks like Rupert Bear!" he said and Electrotaur looked extremely cheesed off. His humming and glowing got louder and quieter and darker and lighter. Jack shot an alarmed look at their bedroom door.

"Shhhh!" he urged. "You'll wake Mum and Dad!"

The humming, thankfully, settled down. There was an awkward silence. Finally Jack said, "Um . . . what do you want?"

Slashermite looked confused and slightly hurt. As if they ought to *know* what he wanted. Electrotaur was more direct. He glared at Jack and declared: "I THIRST!"

19

"OK. . ." said Jack. "You want a drink. No problem." He picked up the plastic beaker of water that Mum always left on the bedside shelf for him. He stretched out his arm as far as it would go and offered the water to Electrotaur. Electrotaur was lifting his lightning fingers to collect it when Lewis suddenly shouted, "NO!" and dived out of his bed, knocking the beaker out of Jack's hands.

"Wha—?" gasped Jack as the water soaked into the carpet and then he realized. Electrotaur was full of *electricity*! A beaker of water would be a disaster to him – and everyone within thirty feet of him. Boiling liquid would spurt in all directions, bolts of lightning would bowl across the ceiling and crack all the glass – and everyone's hair would stand on end and catch on fire. Jack knew this kind of thing. He had drawn it only last week for Magnetimite.

"Blimey!" he said.

"You should *remember* what you've made up!" reproved Lewis, clambering shakily back up on to his bunk.

"Oh *blimey!*" said Jack, again, smacking his forehead.

"What does he drink?" asked Slashermite. He had begun nervously scratching his claws up and down the wooden bed posts.

"About ten thousand volts a day," moaned Jack. "Pure electricity! We're not going to get *that* in a can with two straws!"

"I THIRST!" insisted Electrotaur, beginning to pulsate again.

Jack and Lewis and Slashermite looked at each other fearfully. What on earth were they going to do?

"I know!" said Lewis, suddenly. "Our electricity comes in through the sockets! Maybe he can get a drink from there."

Jack looked doubtful. "It sounds a bit dangerous to me," he said, but Electrotaur was glaring at him again and there was no let up with all the blue flashing and humming.

"OK, then," he said. "Lewis and Slashermite, stay over there on the bed. Electrotaur," he leaned down and flicked the "on" switch on the socket behind the door. "Stick your fingers in there! Lewis! Don't you *ever* copy this."

Lewis said, "I'm not an idiot, you know!"

Electrotaur strode across the room, his tail flicking from side to side, sending showers of sparks left and right. He connected his lightning bolt fingers with the socket. A brighter blue wave of power ran up Electrotaur's arm, across his leathery

21

chest, up his other arm, channelled through his fingers and then shot, in a narrow jet, right into his mouth. Electrotaur *drank* electricity in great thrumming gulps. This went on for half a minute and then there was a *ping*, the bedside lamp blinked out and everything went quiet.

Electrotaur's humming had now settled to a steady hiss and his blue glow was more even. The sparks in his eyes and on the tips of his fingers died down. He sighed. "ALL GONE," he said. He was certainly right. In the road outside every street lamp and every window was dark.

"Can he go now?" whispered Jack, who was now

22

bunched up in the ragged duvet with Lewis and Slashermite. "He's not still thirsty, is he?"

"I HAVE DRUNK," said Electrotaur. "IT IS GOOD. BUT SOON, I THIRST AGAIN."

Jack stared at the others, now lit only with Electrotaur's glow. "There's no more power *in* this house. There's none in half the street! Maybe the doughnuts will help – he *eats* doughnuts – but mostly he drinks electricity. Flippineck! Why couldn't I have made him drink orange squash?"

With a sudden thought, Jack peered at Slashermite, who guiltily snapped his claws shut again, having been stabbing absent-mindedly at Lewis's pillow.

"What do *you* drink?" he asked, narrowing his eyes first at the small monster and then at his creator. Lewis looked awkward.

"A fine golden liquid," began Slashermite, but Lewis flapped his hands at his creation and shook his head urgently.

"Lewis!" Jack yanked his brother round by the collar of his pyjama top. "You *didn't!*"

Lewis looked *very* awkward. "Well, how was *I* to know?"

Slashermite stared at each boy, confused. "I drink we—"

 23

"Wee-bley's finest apple juice!" cut in Lewis. "That's what you drink!"

"Oh," said Slashermite. "Well. That will do nicely. I *am* thirsty. And hungry too. I will need to eat and drink before we leave."

Jack was giving Lewis another dark look. "Lewis? Wee-bley's finest apple juice?! What does he *eat*? Tell me now!"

"P—" began Slashermite and Jack gave a shout of disgust.

"—orridge," finished Slashermite.

"Porridge! Porridge!" repeated Lewis, indignantly.

Jack felt slightly bad for thinking the worst, until Slashermite added. . .

"With ants in."

Jack groaned. "OK, so when you've had your food and drink, will you be going?"

Slashermite looked surprised and hurt again. "Of course," he said. "After we have completed our quest."

Chapter Four

The Holes

"*What* quest?!" asked Jack.

"The quest you brought us here for," replied Slashermite.

Jack and Lewis looked at each other. Lewis shrugged and pulled a "don't look at *me*" kind of face.

"Um. . ." began Jack.

"But before we stride out upon our quest," said Slashermite, sounding just like Lewis when he was playing *knights and dragons*, "I shall need to eat and drink. Where is this Weebley's finest apple juice and ant porridge kept?"

Sorting out the Weebley's was easy. Their mum always kept a good stock of apple and orange juice in the fridge. Ant porridge, though, was a little harder to sort out.

"*You* are on ant collection duty!" whispered Jack,

moving his torchlight across the larder shelves in search of porridge oats. Lewis pulled a face. "Don't you look at *me* like that! You're the one who came up with ant porridge – you can blummin well sort out the ants."

"Well, when I thought up what he ate I didn't expect Merrion's Mead to bring him to *life!*" Lewis muttered and drew back the bolts on the kitchen door.

"Do you think that's what's happened?" asked Jack, remembering their aunt's gift for the first time.

"Well, yeah – obviously!" said Lewis. "We were sort of dreaming about Taurs and then we spilled the mead on them – well, *you* did – and now they're real. Just like Lord Merrion's dreams. Makes perfect sense."

"But . . . that was just a story. . ." murmured Jack.

It would have been pitch-black outside, with no nearby street lights left working, but a soft blue glow spilled out of their bedroom window, where Electrotaur stood obediently, back by the radiator. Slashermite was next to him, peering excitedly outside and bouncing up and down.

Lewis stepped across the patio, feeling the cold, damp brick under his bare feet and moved his torch

beam in slow zigzags across it. One or two moths fluttered through the light but Lewis couldn't see any ants. He crouched down for a closer look and then spotted a crumbly mound of soil along the gap of one of the patio flagstones. Aha! Lewis bashed it. Immediately several ants came running out, looking around like angry builders whose new wall has just been flattened. Which of course they were – and it had. Lewis had a mug with him and he quickly swept the ants, crumbly mud and all, into it.

"Got 'em?" asked Jack, quietly, when his brother returned. He was standing at the stove, quietly stirring porridge oats and milk over the blue gas flame. "Good job we don't cook on electricity, isn't it?" he said. "I had to light the gas with a match, like Grandad showed me that time." He shuddered to think about all the rules he was breaking. Messing with electricity sockets, striking matches, bringing monsters to life. . .

Lewis began to fish out the ants and dropped the poor creatures one by one into the porridge. Soon the soggy white mass was speckled with black. "It was quick . . . they wouldn't have felt it," sighed Jack.

With Lewis holding the torches they crept back up the stairs. Jack carried the bowl of ant porridge with a spoon, and a cup of apple juice. Back inside their room, Slashermite scampered eagerly across to them. "Sit down," said Jack, sounding just like their mother. Slashermite did. "Cross legs," added Jack and Slashermite did, swiping crescent moons into the carpet with his razor-sharp toenails. Jack handed him the ant porridge and apple juice and Slashermite began his first meal with great gusto.

"I'm afraid we haven't got any doughnuts" Jack told Electrotaur anxiously. "But I will get you some soon." Electrotaur nodded and said nothing.

Slashermite was making small noises of contentment as he slurped the ant porridge off his spoon. "Nois-y!"

28

reproved Jack, and their guest looked embarrassed and slurped more quietly. Jack pulled Lewis back on to the lower bunk and spoke to him quietly. "What are we going to do about this quest business? What quest are they *on*?"

Lewis shrugged. "I don't know. I didn't make up any quest for Slashermite. I didn't get that far."

"Just as well," said Jack, darkly, thinking about Slashermite's meal. "I didn't make up anything for Electrotaur either. We're going to have to come up with something though," He flicked his eyes across to the window, where the sky was beginning to get lighter. "And soon! We've got to get them out of here before Mum and Dad wake up. They'll go berserk!"

"Where can we hide them?" hissed Lewis. "They're never going to fit in the shed or behind the garage."

"We have to take them further away than that." Jack bit his lip and thought. "I know! The Holes!"

Lewis nodded slowly. "We'd better get our boots on."

Getting Slashermite and Electrotaur down the stairs and out of the front door was not easy. While Jack and Lewis crept, their nerves jangling with every creak under their feet, Slashermite kept bouncing excitedly up and down and trying to slash the wallpaper, Jack had to seize his little purple wrist several times or the hallway would have been shredded. Electrotaur just *buzzed* so loudly. "Shhhh!" said Jack. Finally they reached the door, unbolted it, and got outside.

There was a small wood close to where they lived. They called it the Holes because inside the wood were large mounds of earth, which must have been dumped there many years ago. The mounds were now covered in bushes and brambles, but in them were a dozen child-sized holes, dug into the sides like small caves. Jack reckoned they'd been made by children years and years ago, when the soil was freshly dug and only just dumped there. Now they were hard earth, held firm by a network of roots.

The peculiar party of two small boys in pyjamas, coats and Wellingtons, one short purple monster with razor-sharp claws and one eight foot golden monster with sparks coming out of him, sidled down a narrow cut way between two houses. This led into a patch of muddy car park, which in turn led to a wall of trees; the edge of the Holes. The wood looked very different in the dark, but smelled very much the same.

"This is it," said Jack, waving his dimming torch light towards the thickest part of the bushes. "Not many people know about this one."

Giving Lewis his torch to hold, he ducked under a branch and began to swipe some dead leaves and twigs to one side, revealing some rusty corrugated iron. "Yes!" said Jack. "Nobody else has been here!" He dragged the wobbly metal panel to one side, and beneath it was another hole – but this was a really big and deep one, which curved smoothly inwards like a basin. It was easily big enough for three or four children and its walls were firm and strong. Jack would never have allowed Lewis into a crumbly, unstable hole. He had heard about them collapsing on people. "Me and Lewis found it last summer," he said, "It's quite safe."

Slashermite scampered down into the hole and looked around it cheerfully as Lewis shone the torch in after him. Electrotaur followed stiffly, bending over to fit inside. He didn't look impressed.

"OUR QUEST BEGINS HERE?" he queried, as Slashermite ran his claws along the damp earth wall and beamed with pleasure at the pattern he was making.

"Er – yes," said Jack. "Your quest is to be very quiet in this hole."

Both monsters now looked very unimpressed. It didn't sound quite as thrilling as seeking out the Sapphire Sphere of Destiny or the Fantastic Fork of Fate or beating back the Bludgeoning Boulders of Baggadagga.

"THIS IS A QUEST?" asked Electrotaur. Jack shuffled his feet. "Well – it's a *starter* quest. A kind of . . . practice quest. To get you prepared. We must leave you here now, for a while, but we will come back when it's light, and we will tell you about your proper quest."

"WHY NOT NOW?" asked Electrotaur. Jack wished he'd created a more agreeable character, like Slashermite. Still, he might have spilled the mead on Grippakillataur and that would've been *very* bad news.

"Because I may not – er – reveal this quest unto you before the break of day and the rising of the sun, Electrotaur," said Jack. Lewis continued. . .

"Stay where thou art, Tauronians," he proclaimed. Jack pulled a face at him and mouthed "where thou *art?!*" in disbelief, but Lewis swept on. "The time will be upon us soon enough, to reveal to you the quest for which you have been called.

But for now you must rest and prepare – for we will need you both to be at the peak of your powers. Stay here – reveal yourselves to no one. When we return we will be singing the Tauronian Battle Song, and by this you will know us."

Jack gaped at his brother, impressed. "We'll pull the metal cover back when we get out," he said. "Not all the way though – so you can get some air and see

 33

when it's light. If anyone comes, though, pull it right over if you can and keep quiet."

As they scrambled back down the other side of the Holes, leaving their creations sitting obediently in their small cave, Jack peered at Lewis with a look of amazement. "*The Tauronian Battle Song?* Blimmineck, Lew! I hope you can make one up – and sharpish!"

"I can," said Lewis.

"Anyway, making up songs is the least of our problems," said Jack as they walked back up through the cut way. "What about this quest? We can't just leave them there waiting for ever. What if Electrotaur starts to THIRST again? And he'll get hungry too. We'll have to get doughnuts."

"And batteries," said Lewis and Jack gave him a thump. "Brilliant idea! Batteries *are* just little cans of electricity, after all," he said.

As they let themselves quietly back into the house, everything was still. In their bedroom Lewis flicked the light switch and nothing happened. "Still no electricity," muttered Jack, quietly. "I wonder how much he drank? A whole street's worth, by the looks of it." The street lights were also still out.

"We've got to go to the shops," said Lewis, emptying his piggy bank with little clinks. "Before

Mum and Dad wake up. We haven't got much time."

He was right. Jack seized his own money box and he and Lewis began to quickly count how much they had, by torchlight. Together they worked out they had £15.28. Not bad. Some of Jack's birthday money and some recent tooth fairy payments for Lewis.

"There's that shop on Bridge Way," Jack told Lewis. "It's open all night. If we go now, we can be back with doughnuts and batteries before Mum and Dad wake up. We'd better put proper clothes on, though."

They quickly changed into jeans, jumpers and trainers and then crept back down the stairs for the third time that night. As soon as they were beyond the front gate they broke into a run and pelted down past the darkened houses until they reached the part where the lights were still on. Around two corners and past the park, they found the twenty-four-hour convenience shop. It was brightly lit and one or two customers were milling around inside. Jack led the way to the bakery section. They scanned the shelves for doughnuts. "Jam or iced?" asked Lewis.

"Either," said Jack. "I didn't say which. No – hang on – ring doughnuts. He'll get all messy with jam or icing sugar." They filled a bag with ring doughnuts, still warm from the early morning bakery. "You get six for ninety-nine pence," said Jack. "So I think we can do twelve. Ten for Electrotaur and one each for us. I'm starving."

The batteries were kept in packs behind the till. A pasty-faced girl in a striped tunic stood there, looking bored. "How many batteries can we buy for – um – £13.30?" asked Jack, after a quick calculation. The girl stared at them. "What kind?" she asked, dully.

"Well – er – what have you got?" She stared at him a moment longer, and then said "Double A, triple A, Cs or Ds. What's it for?"

"A bad-tempered eight foot electricity-drinking monster," said Jack.

"You being funny?" She folded her arms and pursed her lips. "Where's your mum?" she asked. "You shouldn't be out in the middle of the night on your own."

Jack felt a stab of panic, but Lewis said, "She's over there." He pointed to a woman, about their mum's age, who was leaning against the doorway, smoking a cigarette. She wore a skirt way shorter than the ones their mum wore. She was also, clearly, a bit drunk.

The girl behind the till suddenly looked sorry for them. "Look," she said. "These are on special offer." She pulled out two boxes of double A batteries in sets of twelve. They looked like a cheap make, thought Jack, but Electrotaur wouldn't know the difference.

"You can afford these – and one C," said the girl, taking a larger, barrel-shaped battery off the stand, too. She rang in the prices on the till. It came to £12.97. Plus £1.98 for the doughnuts. They even got thirty-three pence change.

"Thanks!" beamed Jack. He'd never been so excited about batteries before. As they ran past the woman in the doorway, Lewis shouted over his shoulder "Come on, Mum!" She stared after them but didn't – fortunately – follow. They giggled all the way back to their house, each stuffing a doughnut.

"This is brilliant!" said Jack, as they reached their gate.

But exactly one second later he wasn't so sure. As the sun broke over the horizon there was a loud boom. In the pale golden sky above the Holes rose a plume of smoke. . .

Chapter Five

Smoking Doughnuts

Jack and Lewis stared at each other in horror. "Electrotaur!" Jack clutched his brother's arm. Within seconds windows were opening and the people were peering out to see what was going on. "Quick!" hissed Lewis. "We've got to get back to the Holes before anyone sees us out here!"

They ducked into their front garden, keeping low, and ran into the side passage that led to the back garden just as the front bedroom window was pushed open and their dad's sleepy, bothered face appeared. Fortunately he was looking up into the sky and didn't see them.

"Go! Go!" gasped Jack. In two minutes they reached the edge of the wood and began to hurtle noisily through it, the bag of doughnuts jumping around in Lewis's hands and the batteries

38

thudding against Jack's chest. What had Electrotaur done? Had he just exploded? thought Jack, feverishly. He tried to remember if he had made up a bit about his monster which meant he might explode at any time, but really, he'd made up so many of the creatures he called Taurs that he couldn't possibly keep all their details in his head.

Soon they reached the Holes and the bit of corrugated iron, which should have been concealing their creations from view. But it lay a few feet away from the little cave, upended against a knot of brambles. Jack shouted, "Electrotaur! Slashermite! Where are you?!" They were not there.

Lewis gave a shout, "look!" He pointed to some recently slashed rhododendron bushes. Slashermite might as well have taken a ball of bright orange string and fed it out behind them. The trail of slashes was easy to follow. They raced down the woody slope and across a shallow brown stream which wound through the wood, dammed here and there by chunks of old concrete, the odd tyre and a rusty old pram. The pram had a very prominent set of slashes, gleaming silver amid the dull red rust.

 39

"This way!" shouted Lewis. Jack feared for the state of the doughnuts. They'd be totally mashed at this rate. In the distance he could hear fire engine sirens. "Oh no," he moaned as they crashed on through the wood. As they followed more slashes in the trunks of trees, Jack suddenly realized where they were going. A quarter of a mile away, rising from the trees, was a towering metal pylon. It supported a network of cables high in the air. Thousands of volts of electricity poured through it day and night – it was one of those things which grown ups tell you *never* to go near. You could get frazzled like a bit of toast if you did. Today it looked like something *had* got frazzled. The cloud of smoke hid the top of the pylon from view.

The trail of slash marks led them directly to the pylon, which rested its four huge metal feet on a concrete square in the middle of a fenced clearing in the trees. Crouched unhappily at one of these

feet was Slashermite. Jack and Lewis quickly climbed the wooden fencing, with its big yellow warning signs, and Slashermite crouched even lower and started to moan. "I'm sorry, I couldn't stop him! I tried but he just wouldn't listen . . . he was thirsty again – and hungry. I told him we must wait for the Tauronian Battle Song but, oh, what has he done? What has he done?"

Jack and Lewis drew to a halt by edge of the concrete, staring, aghast, at Slashermite. Then they both raised their eyes fearfully up the metal tower until they found Electrotaur, clinging, frozen, halfway up. High up above him, the top of the pylon was making unsteady buzzing and crackling noises, and a small blue-and-yellow blaze whipped around it like a fiery whirlwind.

"Electrotaur! Get down from there this minute!" shouted Jack. Electrotaur looked down at him and a forlorn shower of sparks came out of his tail. He seemed to be shaking his head. "You can't have any more to drink! You'll knock out all the electricity in town!" shouted Jack. "Come on now, before I get cross!" What exactly he'd *do* when he got cross, Jack didn't know. How did you punish an eight foot tall electricity monster? Send it to the naughty corner?

"He's scared," said Lewis and Slashermite nodded. "Yes," he said. "He went up to drink and then the tower ka-boomed at him, and he climbed halfway down again and then had a panic attack."

Jack stared at Slashermite in amazement. "Taurs have *panic attacks?*"

Lewis began to shake the bag of doughnuts. "Come on, Electrotaur! Come on! Lovely doughnuts down here – look!" He opened the top of the bag and the sugary rings sent up a lovely smell. Electrotaur still clung, frozen, to the side of the pylon, but his head tipped down to look at them. "Come *on!*" coaxed Lewis. "Look – they're

42

yummy!" He pulled a ring doughnut out and waved it high in the air. "And they're quite safe," he added.

Electrotaur looked up at the fire and then down at the small boy and the ring doughnut. "We can't climb up!" shouted Jack. "We'll be toasted." He could already feel his hair trying to rise off his scalp, and thought that Electrotaur had probably charged up the air around them tremendously. It had a scary, hot smell. Electrotaur loosened his grip and leaned out a little to get a better look at his breakfast. "I HUNGER!" he said.

"Well, get down here then," snapped Jack. He could hear the sirens getting louder. Lewis was still shaking the doughnut in the air. At last Electrotaur began to move, climbing steadily down the ladder of grey steel girders. In half a minute he was on the ground and Lewis handed him the bag of doughnuts. Electrotaur sat down on the edge of the concrete to eat them and a rather pleasant smell of burnt sugar wafted around him as he munched.

"Oh no, sparky boy!" said Jack. "We can't wait here! Trouble is on the way." He could hear shouts at the edge of the wood, now. "We can't go back the way we came," he said, peering around desperately.

"That's OK – we need to go this way," said

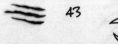

Lewis, pointing in the opposite direction.

"Why that way?" asked Jack, but Lewis shook his head impatiently. "That's the way Aunt Thea lives – obviously." He started to walk and Slashermite stepped out obediently next to him and then scrambled over the fence alongside him. "C'mon," he said again to Electrotaur and this time the Taur rose up, still consuming his doughnuts from an increasingly charred bag, and thudded along beside him. He stepped over the fence easily while Jack climbed. Jack didn't think to ask Lewis if he knew where he was going. Lewis never got lost. His little brother had the most amazing memory and an incredible sense of direction. Everywhere he went, his mind seemed to make a little map and then keep it in a handy place in his head.

Jack hurried Electrotaur along behind Lewis and Slashermite and they were only just in time. "Go! Go! Go!" he hissed, wishing he dared to shove. They got into the cover of the trees two seconds before three burly firefighters vaulted over the wooden fence around the pylon, despite the heavy equipment bags on their backs.

"Oy!" shouted one. Jack glanced back with a twinge of panic, but one of the men was simply

standing, puzzled, holding up a lightly smoking half of a ring doughnut.

They trekked on through the northern end of the woodland as quietly as possible – which wasn't very quiet. Electrotaur marched heavily, crashing and bashing while Slashermite scampered, sending dry leaves in all directions and continually slashed the tree trunks as he went. "Do you *have* to keep doing that?" reproved Lewis. "You're wrecking this place!"

Slashermite looked stricken and folded his claws away instantly. "It's a nervous thing," he said.

Lewis sighed. "You *can't* do it when we get to Aunt Thea's house!"

"Who is this Aunt Thea?" asked Slashermite.

"She's possibly the only grown-up we know who won't faint when she sees you two," said Jack. "No!" he looked sternly at Electrotaur, who had just thrown down the charred, crumpled remains of the empty doughnut bag. "We do *not* drop litter in the woods!" he added. "Pick it *up!*" Electrotaur stopped. His green eyes went purple, and Jack wondered if he'd just pushed his creation too far, but then Electrotaur bent over and picked up the bag. Jack held out his hand and gestured impatiently and a screwed-up paper ball was placed

45

carefully in his palm, along with a small static shock. "Thank you," said Jack, primly, and they went on their way.

It took about ten minutes to get to Aunt Thea's by car, and half an hour through the woodland. There was only one problem with taking the woodland route; a problem which meant they rarely went that way unless it was a dry summer. As they reached the edge of the wood, the problem flowed past them in a gentle curve. In a dry spell the river fell low enough to reveal a number of pebbly islands, which made natural stepping stones. Unfortunately it had been raining quite a lot recently, and the river was high and busy. Only feet away from its far bank stood the pretty row of stone cottages where Aunt Thea lived. Everything was quiet and nobody seemed to have been woken by the exploding pylon.

"Come on," said Lewis, as they stood on the bank. "We'll just have to wade across."

He picked up a stick and prodded out as far across as he could reach, trying to work out how deep the water was. Slashermite and Electrotaur watched, fascinated. They had never seen a river before. Electrotaur copied Lewis as he put an exploratory toe in the water.

46

"It's not *very*—" began Lewis, and then there was a white flash and a sizzling crack and both he and Electrotaur keeled over backwards on to the ground.

Chapter Six

A Bit of a Shock

Jack stood frozen, staring at the two figures lying on the river bank. Lewis's eyes were shut and his hair was sticking out in all directions, like a dandelion clock. His hand still gripped the stick. Electrotaur lay beside him, motionless and silent.

"What has happened? Oh, what has happened to my creator?!" Slashermite scampered across to Lewis before Jack could move again.

"Wait!" Jack heard himself cry, in a dry and raspy voice. He remembered seeing films in school about kids getting electrocuted. They always said you shouldn't touch the victim unless you were sure the electric current had stopped going through them. If it hadn't, you could get shocked too.

Slashermite paid him no attention. His claws folded carefully into his palms, he was gently poking Lewis in the head. Jack ran across, knelt

down and shook his little brother's shoulders. "Lewis! Lew! Wake up!" There was no belt of electricity, just a light tingle along Jack's arms. Lewis's eyes didn't open and Jack desperately put his ear to his mouth, trying to hear or feel if he was breathing. His heart began to screw up inside him with awful fear. He should have looked after Lewis. He was his big brother. How was he ever going to tell Mum and Dad?

Just then, Lewis coughed loudly in Jack's ear and said "—deep." His blue eyes opened and he looked around him in confusion. "How did I get here?" he murmured. Jack shouted out with relief. "Lew! Oh – Lew! We thought you were dead."

Lewis sat up and rubbed his eyes. "You got electrocuted!" said Jack, who felt like crying with relief. "Electrotaur put his toe in the river too!" He gave his brother's head a rough mussing and then an awkward cuddle. Lewis coughed again and shoved him off.

"What's happened to Electrotaur?" he got up, swaying slightly, and went over to the eight foot creature in checked trousers, still lying on the bank.

"Don't touch him!" shouted Jack and Slashermite, at the same time. Lewis crouched

down next to Electrotaur, but he didn't touch.

"I think he's still alive," he said. "We just need to wake him up. Have you got those batteries, Jack?" Jack pulled the bag of batteries out from where they'd been jammed, down his sweatshirt. "Let's just try a little one," said Lewis, and picked up a thick twig from the ground near Electrotaur. Jack passed him a small double A battery, and Lewis split the stick and then shoved the battery sideways into the fork of it. It held quite well.

"No!" he said, firmly. "I'm the eldest! I'm not risking you getting electrocuted again." Then he gritted his teeth, reached over, and touched the battery to Electrotaur's mouth. As first, nothing happened. At least nobody got electrocuted. Then, after a few seconds, there was a small, dry click and then Electrotaur began to gently hum again.

"Brilliant!" murmured Jack. "I think we've switched him back on!"

Electrotaur opened his brilliant green eyes and turned his head towards Jack. "I SLEPT," he said.

"Yeah," said Jack. "You slept. But it's time to wake up now. We've got to get going!"

"But how?" asked Lewis, as Electrotaur sat up, groggily. "We can't let him near the river again. We

 50

have to make a bridge of some kind – some planks or an old door – something like that."

They scanned the river bank and the woods behind them but there was nothing as helpful as an old door or a plank of wood. Jack made a decision. "We'll have to leave him here while we go over to Aunt Thea's. She'll have something we can use."

Lewis looked at Electrotaur, doubtfully. "But what if he goes wandering off again – like last time?" He eyed the sky over the trees behind them. There were still traces of smoke away to the west.

Jack turned to Electrotaur, who was now back up on his feet. He used his most masterful voice. "Electrotaur, I am your creator, and you must do as I say – is that not so?"

Electrotaur stared at him, unblinking, and then nodded. "I MUST," he said.

"Then go to the centre of these bushes," Jack pointed back into the wood, "and stay there, completely still, until we come back for you. OK?" Electrotaur just stared at him. Jack bit his lip with worry and then added: "It's part of your quest – do you understand?"

"I DO," said Electrotaur and he went straight into the bushes, crashing his way right into the thickest, darkest part, and then sank down, cross-

legged, among the dry leaves and roots. All that could be seen of him was the occasional blue spark.

Jack, peered in through the bushes, which were fortunately quite damp and unlikely to catch fire. "You need to keep perfectly still – it's – er – another part of your quest! And you'll mess up the big quest if you wander off again. Try not to hum too loudly." Electrotaur's hum dropped down a little in volume. "We'll be back to get you as soon as we can," said Jack, feeling strangely sorry for the monster, sitting forlornly in a bush. He pushed the packet of batteries in towards him. "In case you thirst," he said. Electrotaur nodded and went back to keeping still and not humming too loudly.

Jack and Lewis decided to just wade through the river, each holding one of Slashermite's wrists. He was quite warm to the touch and his skin was very smooth under their fingers, like soft plastic. As they scrambled up the opposite bank, Slashermite shook himself like a dog and the water flew off his chunky legs and unfinished tail.

"C'mon," said Jack in a low voice and then walked up Aunt Thea's path and pressed the brass button on her red-painted door. A bell jangled softly on the other side and they waited. At first

there was no response
and Jack had a terrible
thought that perhaps
she'd gone away
again. But as he
pressed the button a
second time the door
opened a crack, a taut
brass chain holding it
to the frame. Aunt
Thea's sleepy face
peered through the
crack.

"Lewis?" she murmured in surprise. "Jack? What on earth are you doing here at this hour? Is everything all right?" Suddenly, she fumbled to get the chain off and open the door. "Has there been an accident? Is it an emergency?"

"Well, kind of," said Jack, aware of Slashermite bouncing nervously behind him. "We had a kind of accident with the Merrion's Mead. And we've had a few emergencies since then."

"What do you mean?" Aunt Thea, in her green silk dressing gown, scrubbed the sleep out of her eyes.

"Well – you see – we were drawing Taurs; and I

53

knocked the mead all over them, and then they came to life," explained Jack.

"Then Electrotaur drank all the electricity in the house," went on Lewis. "And we had to make ant porridge for Slashermite – and he *wrecked* the place!

"So then," said Jack, "we had to hide them in the Holes, and get some batteries and doughnuts, but Electrotaur drank a pylon until it exploded and now he's hiding in a bush because he can't get across the river so we need a plank or a door, to get him across."

"Jack – Lewis," said Aunt Thea, gently. You can tell me and I won't be cross. Did you actually *drink* the Merrion's Mead?"

Jack and Lewis looked at each other and then stood aside so Aunt Thea could see Slashermite, who grinned at her nervously and decapitated the potted geraniums in her porch.

Aunt Thea fell into her elephant's foot umbrella stand.

Chapter Seven

A Door for a Taur

Aunt Thea lay among the blue, green, red and tartan assortment of umbrellas, gripping the curved leather handle of one of them very hard as she stared at Slashermite in disbelief. Eventually, Jack stepped into the hallway and sank to his knees to pat her on the forehead. She felt a little clammy.

"It's OK, Aunty, really. His name's Slashermite and he's not dangerous. He's a goodie. Lewis drew him."

Aunt Thea's eyes remained locked on the little purple creature bouncing up and down on her front step. Slashermite gave her a watery smile. Aunt Thea picked up the tartan umbrella and cracked herself on the head with it, quite hard. They all winced. "Nope," she said. "Definitely awake."

"Come on, Aunty!" said Jack. You always say we

 55

should try to believe at least six impossible things before breakfast." Aunt Thea narrowed her eyes at him and then nodded.

"I do say that, don't I. . .?" she murmured.

"Yes – and it *is* before breakfast. In fact – I'd say it's about time for breakfast, wouldn't you?" She nodded some more and sat up. "We're all starving," went on Jack. "And Slashermite likes

porridge. Could you do him some porridge? Then we can tell you all about it."

Aunt Thea took a deep breath and got to her feet. "Porridge I can definitely do," she said.

"But. . ." added Jack, feeling a bit awkward. "Before the porridge, could you let us have a door?"

"Or a ladder," added Lewis, chirpily.

Aunt Thea shook her head and took a deep breath and said, in a much steadier voice, "So let me get this straight – you've created a character out of pens and paper and spilled magic mead on it; it's come to life and now you've brought it here for porridge *and* – a door."

Jack nodded.

"Any particular kind of door?" queried Aunt Thea. "A back door, a front door, one with a bell? A double-glazed patio door? What do you think I am – Homebase?"

Lewis came in, holding Slashermite by the wrist. "Blades *in*," he muttered and Slashermite obediently tucked them away. "It's like this, Aunty," he said. "I put my toe in the river and then Electrotaur, that's the other monster, copied me and we both got shocked. That's why my hair's like this."

His aunt surveyed his dandelion clock hair,

which was slowly beginning to flatten down again, but still made him look a bit like a mad professor. "Lewis – are you all right?" she said, suddenly sounding much more normal.

"Yes, I'm fine," said Lewis. "But Electrotaur isn't. He's hiding in a bush because we can't get him over the river to your house. We need to get a door or a ladder or something to make a bridge."

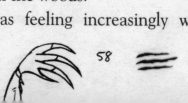

"I see," said Aunt Thea. "Well – as it happens, I think I may have just the thing in my shed."

It was an old panelled door, painted white and still attached to its slightly rusting hinges. "Always thought this might be handy," said Aunt Thea, as she hauled it out of the shed. "You know, for rescuing mythical beasts from the woods."

Jack was feeling increasingly worried about

Electrotaur. "We've really got to go now," he said. "I think he'll stay where he was told, but he might start to thirst again."

"Well, he can have a drink when he gets back here," said Aunt Thea. Lewis and Jack exchanged glances, but decided to tell her exactly *what* Electrotaur drank later.

Holding the door between them, Jack, Lewis and Aunt Thea edged carefully out of the house. Fortunately it wasn't yet six o'clock on a Sunday, and most people would still be asleep. Slashermite had agreed to wait in the back garden, under cover of a high hedge and an old apple tree, in case any neighbour should happen to look out of their back windows. He'd promised not to slash anything. He was on a "not slashing things quest" said Lewis.

They quickly found the narrowest point of the river and Jack stepped into it, hauling one end of the door across with him, while Lewis and Aunt Thea steadied the other end and pushed it down on to the bank. Lewis ran across it easily, and Aunt Thea, in her dressing gown and wellies followed more sedately. Jack led the way back into the woods, his trainers and socks squelching, listening for the low hum of Electotaur. He was filled with relief when he spotted a dim blue glow

 59

in the tangle of branches and called quietly, "Electrotaur! We're back. You can come out now."

Electrotaur didn't move, but the humming got slightly louder and the blue grew brighter. "C'mon – out you come," coaxed Jack. But Electrotaur stiffly shook his big head.

"I FEAR," he said.

"It's all right!" said Jack, holding back some prickly holly branches and waving Electrotaur through them. "It's only Aunty Thea. She's a friend – aren't you, Aunty?" Aunt Thea nodded faintly, staring at Electrotaur with her mouth open. He certainly was an impressive sight. Pulses of darker blue ran across his chest and shoulders in waves, like an electrical sea, and his green eyes glowed almost ultraviolet. He was dazzling and fortunately, sitting down, you didn't really notice the trousers.

"I FEAR," he said again, and he really did sound scared, thought Jack.

"What? What do you fear?" Jack asked.

Electotaur stared back at him. "MEN COME. MEN COME NOW! I HEAR!" At this moment Lewis and Aunt Thea both gave a cry of panic. They were staring deep into the woods and now Jack could hear the approach of what sounded like

several men yomping along heavily amid the trees.

"It's the firefighters!" squeaked Lewis. "We've got to get him out of here! Now!"

Jack snapped his attention back to Electrotaur. "ELECTROTAUR!" he said, in a masterly but not too loud voice. "I am your creator and I COMMAND you to get up and follow me ... FAST!"

This, thank goodness, did the trick. The eight foot, golden buzzing beast got to his feet and ducked out from the holly bushes. Jack seized him by the hand without thinking and felt a mild shock through the jagged fingers – but only like the static from a nylon carpet – and then they began to run. They all crashed back through the woods, hearing the yomping men getting closer. There was a shout from one of them, and then they sounded as if they were running too.

"They must be trying to find out who messed with the pylon," puffed Jack, feeling a bit like the weirdest ever version of Jack and Jill as he loped along hand in hand with Electrotaur.

"Pylon? What pylon? Who messed with a pylon?" Aunt Thea puffed back.

Jack said nothing, but glanced over his shoulder. He could make out a gleam of fluorescent-yellow

uniform two hundred metres behind them. "Oy!" someone shouted. "Hold on there!"

"It was the smoking doughnut!" burbled Lewis, sprinting ahead of them. "They found the smoking doughnut and now they know someone was there!"

"Smoking. . .?" Aunt Thea began and then shook her head and just ran faster. They skidded across the muddy bank and nearly toppled straight into the river. Jack saved Electrotaur at the last moment, and then steered him quickly on to the door.

Electrotaur began to freeze with fear as he saw the water, but Jack pulled up his most impressive creator voice and hissed: "MOVE! DO AS I COMMAND!" The creature stumbled forward and was on the other bank in two lopes of his long legs. They hurtled along with him, pelted across Aunt Thea's little garden and all hit her front door with a big *whump*! There was an agonising and terrifying moment as she fumbled for her key and the voices behind them got louder. "You there!" bellowed one of them and they shrank together and twisted around fearfully – but whoever had yelled had not yet emerged from the trees.

"Quick! Quick!" squeaked Jack and Lewis and at last Aunt Thea got the key into the lock with her

trembling hand and turned it. They all fell into her hallway in a shower of blue sparks and then scrambled along its polished wooden floor. Aunt Thea leaped to her feet and grabbed the door. She had the good sense not to slam it, but swiftly and quietly shut it.

"Stay there!" she said and bounded into her front room to peer between the curtains.

"Did they see us?" gasped Lewis. "Are they coming?"

Aunt Thea watched, holding the curtains closed and just squinting through a tiny crack. "Shhhh!" she said. "They've come over the river and they're going door to door. I think you'd all better hide. Get the other one in from the garden, Lewis. Jack – open the door under the stairs."

"We'll never all fit in there," said Jack, as Lewis crept through the kitchen and opened the back door quietly.

"Just do it," said Aunt Thea, still spying through the curtains. "Looks like they're going to knock the doors. Oh dear. We've probably got about a minute before they get to us."

Lewis returned with Slashermite, who looked relieved to see his fellow Taur, as Jack opened the cupboard under the stairs. Except that it *wasn't* a

cupboard under the stairs. To his immense surprise, instead of a vacuum cleaner, lightbulbs and stacks of old newspapers, a set of stone steps led down into a cellar. His flicked a switch above his head and a soft yellow lit the gloom below.

"Hurry up," said Aunt Thea, from the front room. She had stopped looking through the curtains and was taking off her Wellingtons and hiding them behind the sofa. Jack sent Slashermite, Lewis and Electrotaur down the steps. Electrotaur had to bend over almost in half to fit. Then Jack shut the door behind him, but could not resist pausing and peering through the crack at its hinges. Just as he did there was a knock at the door. Aunt Thea did not go to it immediately. She waited until it was knocked again, louder, and a muffled male voice shouted "Open up please – fire and rescue service!" Then he caught a glimpse of her, wrapping her gown more tightly around her and shuffling barefoot across the hallway. He heard her fumbling with the security chain and re-attaching it, and then opening the door as far as it would allow.

"Sorry to disturb you, madam," came the voice, much more clearly now. "There's been an incident with the electricity pylon in the woods – a fire –

and we're concerned that some local youngsters may have been involved."

Jack heard the door being unchained and then his aunt responded in a strange, fluffy, excitable voice, entirely unlike her usual one. "Oh, Officer! How terrible! But how can I help? Would you like a cup of tea?"

"Er – no – thank you, madam, that's very kind, but we just need to ask you a few questions." The firefighter sounded embarrassed and Jack suddenly knew exactly the kind of soppy look his aunt was giving the man.

"What can I possibly tell you?" gasped Aunt Thea, sounding sillier by the moment. "I've been asleep!"

"Well – er – did you happen to hear anything in the last hour or so, madam? Perhaps some kids playing nearby? Or have you noticed any groups of children or teenagers hanging around here recently?"

"No – no, I can't say I have. I would *so* like to help. Perhaps you could give me your number, in case I do notice anything?"

Jack stifled a giggle. He could actually hear Aunt Thea tapping the firefighter on the stiff material of his uniform. The firefighter coughed nervously and said, "Er – just dial your local station, madam. . ." and tramped quickly back down the path. Seconds later the front door closed and Aunt Thea whipped open the cellar door. She didn't look at all surprised to see him there, sniggering. She folded her arms and gave him a *look*.

"Right, you lot!" she said. "Up here, now! I'm going to make you all breakfast – and you're going to tell me *exactly* what you've been up to."

Chapter Eight

Breakfast with Beasts

Aunt Thea refused to put ants in Slashermite's porridge. She found a small plastic tub full of chocolate strands in her cupboard – the kind you put on the top of cakes – and shook those into the oats instead. Slashermite didn't seem to mind. Electrotaur was slightly harder to please. Although he was convinced by the English muffins dipped in caster sugar (they all firmly told him these were another kind of doughnut) there was no getting around the drink problem.

"Would you like a drink too, Electrotaur?" asked Aunt Thea, exactly as if she was hosting a tea party and the eight foot glowing thing with a dragon's head and sparks coming off its tail was just another child.

"Er . . . Aunty. . ." began Jack, nervously, but then Electrotaur noticed the sockets under the wall cupboards and abruptly stood up. "NO!" shouted

Jack, as his creation stepped across the kitchen floor with his hand outstretched towards it.

Electrotaur paused and looked at Jack, rather sulkily. "I THIRST!" he said. But he turned around and sat back down again.

"What *is* going on?" asked Aunt Thea, putting three delicious-smelling bacon sandwiches on the table.

"Well, you see, Electrotaur drinks electricity," mumbled Jack.

"He had a great big drink at our house," chimed in Lewis, excitedly. "Then all the lights went out. In most of the street!"

"He can have these," said Jack, pulling the remaining batteries out from inside his sweatshirt. Aunt Thea, shaking her head in disbelief, picked a tall plastic beaker off the draining board and piled all the batteries into it. Then she placed it carefully in front of her guest.

"Say thanks, Leccy!" grinned Lewis, through a mouthful of crispy bacon and bread.

"THANKS, LECCY," said Electrotaur gravely, and they all burst out laughing. The monster solemnly picked up the beaker and tipped it towards his mouth and there was a metallic clunking as the heavy batteries slid into each other. Electrotaur buzzed more loudly for a few seconds and his tail made a sort of popping noise. He put the beaker down and they saw that the batteries had twisted and pulled inwards, like plastic bottles with the air squeezed out. "THANKS, LECCY," said Electrotaur again, glowing slightly brighter, and began to eat his third sugared muffin.

Aunt Thea sat down with them and picked up her bacon sandwich, still staring at Electrotaur. "Right – from the very beginning," she said, firmly, and took a big bite.

"Well, it started with you," said Jack, and then told her the whole story, beginning with the Merrion's Mead and how it had spilled across their drawings. Aunt Thea listened in awed silence – although she put her hands over her face when they talked about Electrotaur being up the electricity pylon.

"And now they have to do their quest," concluded Jack. "And then they'll be on their way."

"On their way *where* exactly?" asked Aunt Thea. "I can't see them hitchhiking along the M27, can you?"

Jack and Lewis were quiet and Aunt Thea turned to Slashermite, who was happily scraping up the last of the pretend ant porridge, his sharp blade fingers gripping the spoon with some difficulty. "What is your quest, Slashermite?" she asked, kindly.

The little purple beast jiggled in his seat and fixed her with an excited stare. "Master will reveal it to me soon!" he said.

Aunt Thea sighed. "Oh, Lewis. . . Oh, Jack!" she murmured. "You'd better think of a quest for them pretty soon." She looked from Slashermite to Electrotaur and shook her head. "And I don't think making a den or jumping over the shed is going to satisfy these two. They really need a purpose!"

"Why have *we* got to come up with a quest?!" asked Jack, dismayed. "We didn't ask them to come!"

"Yes, you did!" argued his aunt. "That's what Merrion's Mead does! I told you! It makes your dreams come true – and you've been dreaming up Taurs and Mites for as long as I can remember."

"But we didn't drink it!" protested Jack. "We spilled it . . . and anyway, it was all made up really, wasn't it? It was just a story. You didn't believe it either, did you? Not really."

Aunt Thea ate a bit more bacon sandwich and

looked slightly embarrassed. She swallowed and said, "Look, what I said about the little Welsh shop and the mountain and the story of Lord Merrion – that *is* true. The shopkeeper really did tell me that when I bought the bottles. Of course, he didn't tell it quite so *well* as I did, but it *is* the story that goes with the mead. And, as it turns out, it *must* be true." Aunt Thea glanced at the kitchen clock. It was nearly a quarter to seven. "Oh no!" she said again. "Your parents will be mad with worry! I have to phone them!"

"No!" said Jack, alarmed. "What are we going to tell them? They'll never believe it and – and if they do, they'll call the emergency services or something. Slashermite and Electrotaur will be taken away. Electrotaur will go mad! And he'll probably electrocute someone. He can, you know! He's not a baddie – but he can be quite bad-tempered."

"Oh. Great." Aunt Thea looked at Electrotaur warily.

"Mum and Dad sleep for ages on a Sunday, anyway," said Lewis, drinking the last of his warm tea from a big blue mug. "They stay in bed 'til nine if they can. They probably haven't noticed we're not there."

"Nevertheless, we can't risk it. You two must go

 71

home at once – go by the road route in case those firefighters are still searching the woods."

"But – what about. . .?" began Jack.

"Don't worry – your Taurs will be perfectly fine here with me. In fact, I think I'll get Slashermite on a quest to trim my privet hedge. After ten, I'll phone your mum and ask if you can come to lunch. When you come back *make sure* you bring your paper and crayons – the same as you were using yesterday – *and* the bottles of mead."

"But they're empty," said Lewis, forlornly, as she ushered them out of the house.

"Bring them anyway," said his aunt. "And hurry back now! Mind the roads – but *run!*"

They set off at a brisk trot, hot tea and bacon sandwiches bumping along inside them. It was a quarter past seven when they turned into their road. None of the street lights the windows at their end showed any light.

"But they could all just be asleep," murmured Jack, as they quietly lifted the latch and crept back into the hallway. The house was filled with silence and they stood still, listening hard. At length, their father's occasional snores could be heard and they both breathed out in relief. They hadn't been missed. Quietly they tiptoed back upstairs.

Their bedroom was in a terrible state. Fluffy bits of the inside of Lewis's duvet were all over his bed and carpet. He groaned. "I'm going to get the blame!" They both got down on to the floor and started to scoop up the mess. They stuffed the fluff back into Lewis's shredded bedding as best they could. When they thought they'd got all of it up, they carefully rolled the duvet into a big sausage and put it at one end of his bed. There were a few slash marks on the carpet, but they dragged a box of Lego over these.

"What about us?" Lewis looked down at his clothes, which were covered in mud from the woods and the river bank. Jack looked just as bad. Their trainers and socks were still wet. They got out of their clothes, stuffed them in the washing basket in the bathroom, put their trainers by the radiator to dry, had a quick wash and then got back into their pyjamas.

Jack sat on the edge of Lewis's bed and sighed. "Blimey, I'm tired," he said and Lewis yawned widely. "Can I get up with you?" he said. "I can't use my duvet." Jack nodded, yawning too now and they both scrambled up to the top bunk, taking Lewis's pillow, which was only slightly slashed. In minutes, lying head to tail, they were fast asleep.

Chapter Nine

Big Yellow Gnashers

"Jack! Lewis! Wake up, you two." Mum was leaning over the edge of the top bunk, smiling at them. "Why on earth are you both in the same bed?" she asked.

"I had a nightmare," burbled Lewis, sleepily. Jack could hardly open his eyes.

"Oh dear! What was it about?" Mum stroked Lewis's head.

"I dreamt our Tauronian monsters came to life and we had to hide them in the woods and then the big metal thing caught fire and we were chased by men in yellow suits," yawned Lewis and Mum chuckled.

"Funnily enough, there *was* a fire at the pylon in the woods," she said. "It was on the radio this morning. You probably heard me and Dad when we got up in the night to look out of the window.

74

There were firefighters and everything! I expect that's what made you dream of it."

Jack poked his toe hard into Lewis's armpit and Lewis grunted.

"Come on, you two – you don't need *this* much sleep!" said Mum, pulling back the duvet. "You must have been in bed for about fourteen hours!"

"Doesn't seem like it," groaned Jack. Only he and Lewis knew that it was more like six hours at best – and there'd been a lot of running in between.

"Your aunt Thea has just phoned to ask you to come to lunch. Isn't that nice?" said Mum, and they looked at each other, remembering the plan. "Now, come downstairs. I'll do you bacon sandwiches for breakfast."

During their second breakfast that day, eating another round of bacon sandwiches and drinking more warm tea (the power *had* come back on), Jack and Lewis talked quietly whenever Mum left the kitchen.

"We've got to think of a quest," said Lewis, for the third time. They were both silent. Normally they could think up half a dozen quests at any time of the day or night. They loved nothing *more* than thinking up quests.

But it was one thing to *imagine* something . . .

quite another thing to think it up if you knew it might end up *real*. They had just about got away with Electrotaur drinking the local electricity supply and exploding a pylon, but a host of fire-breathing dragons descending on Aunt Thea's back garden for the Taurs to defeat was probably going to get people a bit excited. Even worse, what would you *do* with them all once they'd been slain? Jack didn't think the bin men would take them away without asking a few questions.

They still hadn't thought up a quest by the time they got to Aunt Thea's that lunch time. They had their crayons and paper with them, though, along with the Merrion's Mead bottles, all carefully tucked into Jack's backpack. They half wondered if the Tauronians would still be there. Maybe they wouldn't *last*, said Jack. Perhaps they'd just pop out of existence if he and Lewis weren't there to command them not to.

But Aunt Thea led them straight into the back garden, where Slashermite was neatly trimming the hedges. "Don't they look good?" asked Aunt Thea with great satisfaction. "He's very useful."

Electrotaur wasn't quite as helpful. He was sitting at the far end of the garden, propped against the standing stone. The strange dark red rock

76

stood up like a giant crooked finger, just as it always had done, seeming to beckon at something up in the sky. As well as being the gateway to Tauronia in all their games, Jack also liked to think it was a sort of beacon for aliens.

The stone was taller than their dad, and stood on a slightly raised grassy mound. It was cut from serpentine – a rock which came from Cornwall, Aunt Thea had told them. Fine red veins ran across its blackness. Nobody knew how or when it had been brought from that far away. It took seven hours to get to the serpentine part of Cornwall by car. It must have taken months to get it here by foot, hundreds or even thousands of years ago.

Electrotaur looked quite content, sitting at the base of the standing stone and leaning his back up against it. "How are you, Electrotaur?" asked Jack, kneeling down beside him.

"WELL," said Electrotaur, which was quite a surprise. Nearly everything else he'd said had been about being thirsty or hungry or scared.

Slashermite scampered up behind them, his finger-blades green with grass juice. Behind him Aunt Thea warned: "No!" when he lifted them up towards the serpentine rock. "Slashermite, that is a sacred stone!" she explained. "Nobody slashes it! You may touch it with your blades tucked in." Slashermite nodded and tucked the blades away, before gently nudging the stone with his little purple knuckles. Lewis arrived at the stone, too, and they all sat down, cross-legged, on the grassy mound.

"Lunch is cooking. Cottage pie – lots of it," said Aunt Thea.

"Have you got any more porridge or doughnuts?" asked Lewis.

"Don't need them," said Aunt Thea. "I explained to Slashermite and Electrotaur that while their *favourite* food is doughnuts and ant porridge, you both told me that other foods are just as good for them. They are looking forward to trying my cottage pie."

Jack grinned and nodded, relieved. It was obvious

really! He and Lewis made the rules. Why hadn't he thought of that before?

"So then," said Aunt Thea. "Are you ready to tell us of the quest?"

Jack started to mash up a daisy. He was embarrassed. Then Lewis spoke up.

"We are not yet ready to tell of the quest," he said, in his best medieval knight kind of voice. "The time has not yet come. We must prepare with good food and fine company. Soon, all will be revealed. When you hear the Tauronian Battle Song, it will be time."

An impressed silence followed his words. Jack stared at his little brother with respect. I just hope he's working out a pretty good song, he thought.

They had lunch in the garden, cradling deep dishes of hot cottage pie in their laps. Afterwards, Aunt Thea asked the Taurs to stay outside and took Jack and Lewis to the kitchen table, where she spread out the drawings, crayons, more paper and the bottles of Merrion's Mead. They all sat down and looked at the evidence.

"Hmmm," said their aunt, holding both the pictures up. She raised one eyebrow at Jack. "What were the Rupert Bear trousers about, then?"

Jack blushed. "They were *meant* to look like a

load of flames, sort of criss-crossing around his legs."

"Is that what you *thought* they looked like?" asked Aunt Thea.

"No," mumbled Jack. "I thought they looked like Grandad's golfing trousers."

Aunt Thea peered at the picture and then gave a hoot of laughter. "Yes! So they do! Well, all I can say, Jack, is that it's a *very* good thing you *didn't* draw them better. If you had believed they looked like flames, then Electrotaur would probably be setting fire to my dahlias right now!"

Jack stared at her, realizing what she meant. "So – it's not so much about what we draw as what we *see* in our heads, when we're thinking about them? That's the bit that's come to life?"

"Exactly," said Aunt Thea. "Your creations are made of your thoughts – or dreams. You must have *thought* those fiery legs looked more like your grandad's trousers, or they would, indeed, be a mass of flame. Lucky for us you're not always a *totally* brilliant artist." She turned her attention to Lewis's effort. "And thank goodness Slashermite is basically *you*, Lewis," she said. "You in monster form, that is. No wonder we're getting on together so famously. Shame about his tail though." She pointed

to the drawing, where Slashermite's tail had, well . . . tailed off.

"I would have finished it!" protested Lewis. "But Jack knocked over the mead bottles, and then we went straight up to bed."

"My point is," said Aunt Thea, putting the drawings down and leaning across the table towards them. "If you draw and dream and then spill the mead, you might be able to change that. Sort out Slashermite's tail, for example."

"But there's no mead left! We told you," said Jack. Aunt Thea picked up the bottles and shook them, listening hard. She screwed up her eyes and put her head on one side, holding one finger up for silence. At length she put the bottles down and looked at them thoughtfully. "I think," she said, "there is a tiny bit left in each of them. I'm going to get some boiled water, and we can put just a teaspoon of it in each bottle, then shake it around, and I know it won't be as strong, but it will get nice and meady. Then we can try."

They carefully poured in the boiled water and then resealed the strange twiggy bottles before shaking them thoroughly for two minutes. "Lewis, let's start with Slashermite's tail," said Auth Thea. "You need to finish it – and while you're doing that

I want you to dream up something new about him. Some other power, perhaps. Make it a useful one, eh? Jack and I will leave you to it – you need to concentrate. As soon as you've finished, undo your bottle and tip the mead water all over it."

Lewis picked up a crayon and got started, his small pink tongue poking out of one side of his mouth, and Jack followed Aunt Thea back out into the garden. They found Electrotaur and Slashermite both sitting by the standing stone in the warm spring sunlight. Just as they were about to sit down with them, the most incredible racket started up, crashing through the peace of the Sunday afternoon. Jack jumped and stared around him. It was a roaring, thudding metallic sound that made his heart hammer in his chest.

But Aunt Thea wasn't looking frightened. She was looking furious. "I can't believe the nerve of the man!" she gasped. "On a *Sunday* too! Right! I'm going over there now!"

She turned with a ripple of the silky orange scarf she was wearing across her long brown velvet dress, and stormed back down the garden and into the house. Jack ran after her. "What is it? What is it, Aunty?" he gasped.

"Carry on," called Aunt Thea to Lewis as they

shot through the kitchen and into the hallway. She flung open the front door and strode down the garden path before turning right and marching angrily along the row of little cottages. In the full daylight, Jack noticed something odd about them, which he hadn't seen before. Several of them had curtainless, black windows. The front gardens of these were overgrown with weeds. It seemed that Aunt Thea had lost a few neighbours.

She stalked on down the pavement and then turned abruptly right, along the side passage of one of these empty cottages, muttering furiously under her breath. Jack raced to catch up with her and an extraordinary scene met his eyes when he reached the cottage's back garden.

The garden had once been something very pretty. There were still borders and shrubs and a trellis of honeysuckle clinging to the old brick of the house, but beyond the stone patio was a mess. The old brick wall which had separated the garden from the one next door had been demolished and pieces of it lay in a snake of rubble. Both gardens were full of mounds of earth, brick, chewed-up trees and roots and the winding patterned tracks left by the big yellow digger which was making all the noise. The digger stood, paused, vibrating and roaring

83

with power; its great big shovel, lined with grimy metal teeth, raised in the air.

The reason it was paused, its driver thumping on his controls and shouting bad words that nobody, thankfully, could hear, was that Aunt Thea was now standing directly in its path, her hands on her hips and her gleaming red hair just inches from the base of the giant yellow shovel.

"Try it!" she yelled at the driver. "Just *try it!*"

Chapter Ten

Unpleasant Digs

The digger driver shouted something at Aunt Thea and shook his fist at her like a character from a *Beano* comic. Aunt Thea folded her arms across her chest, planted her feet firmly into the ruined soil, and lifted her chin. The digger driver grappled with the controls of the machine, looking mean and sly.

"Look OUT, Aunty!" shrieked Jack, terribly scared, as the giant yellow shovel lurched upwards, like a fist about to be crashed down. Aunt Thea didn't move. The driver's face grimaced spitefully, and he pulled back a lever in his cab. At once the giant shovel tipped downwards and an avalanche of soil, twigs, leaves, pebbles and grit fell on to Aunt Thea's head.

Jack was enraged. He hurtled across to the digger, leaped into the open side of the cab and grabbed at the driver's head. The driver was totally shocked – he obviously hadn't noticed the boy

 85

watching him – and let out a panicked yelp as Jack yanked him sideways out of the digger. As his feet left the pedals, the digger shuddered into silence and the boy and the man fell on to the ground in a heap, with shouts and curses ringing in the air.

"Get off! Get *off* him, you lout!" bellowed Aunt Thea, wrenching the driver away by his long, greasy hair.

"Oy! He attacked *me*!" The digger driver scrambled to his feet.

"*You* attacked my aunt!" yelled Jack, furiously, getting ready to attack again. Aunt Thea, with bits of garden waste still showering down off her head and shoulders, pulled him to his feet and hugged him.

"Thank you, Jack," she said. "You are a gentleman."

"What is going on here?" bellowed a new voice and Aunt Thea drew herself up, shaking more grit and soil out of her hair as she spun round.

"That's exactly what I came to ask *you*!" she said.

A man had come down the side passage. He was wearing a baggy suit and had egg yolk on his tie. His grey hair was thinning and he obviously hadn't bothered to shave for a few days. He looked at Aunt Thea and then up to the heavens. "Not *you* again," he groaned.

"Yes. Me again," said Aunt Thea. "Now, are you going to tell me what on earth you're doing? One – it's *Sunday*! Two – you don't have permission to crush up these gardens. And three – your scuzzy son just attacked my nephew!"

"He attacked *me*, Dad!" wailed the digger driver

87

again, climbing back into the digger, and looking sulky.

The older man gave his son a look. "A speccy eight-year-old *kid* attacked you?" he asked, sarcastically.

"I'm *not* speccy!" said Jack. He had been wearing his glasses to look at their drawings and now they were hanging slightly sideways off his nose. He put them in his pocket in case he needed to do any more fighting. "And I'm *nine!*"

"Well, if you want to reach ten, you'd better get off my property," said the man.

"It's *not* your property!" hissed Aunt Thea. "You haven't bought it yet!"

"Contracts have been exchanged, Miss Casterbridge, as well you know," sighed the man. "It's as good as done now. No point in beating about the bush."

"Beating about the bush is *exactly* what you are doing! There isn't a bush left standing. You're a vandal! I will contact the council first thing tomorrow and get you stopped, Mr Garsnipe!"

Mr Garsnipe sighed and shoved his hands into the pockets of his old suit. "Miss Casterbridge, why won't you be reasonable? Nearly all of your neighbours have sold or agreed to sell now. At a

very good price, I might add. Why don't you just take the money and go and find another place to live, instead of coming here and making a nuisance of yourself?"

"The only reason anyone has agreed to sell is because you keep bullying them!" said Aunt Thea. "And we both know what will happen once we're all gone. The whole area will get flattened so you can build a great big mass of red brick, with as many tiny flats as you can poke into it and no character at all. And then, of course, there's the standing stone! What will you do with that? Tip it over and turn it into a barbecue?"

Mr Garsnipe laughed. "Do you know something, Miss Casterbridge? Your standing stone, as you call it, isn't even a monument. There's no record of it in the council plans. I heard that it was just planted there by some hippy in the 1960s. It's just a chunk of rock, you silly woman."

Aunt Thea took a deep breath, and led Jack with her, back across the garden. "If I hear any more digging I will call the police," she called over her shoulder. "And I will tell them about your son attacking my nephew and trying to bury me alive. See if I don't!"

Mr Garsnipe's son mumbled something rude.

"Leave it. . ." said his dad, and the two just made do with a menacing stare after Jack and Aunt Thea as they stalked down the passageway. Aunt Thea looked amazingly dignified for a woman covered in mud and sticks, thought Jack.

"What was all *that* about?" asked Jack, picking some twigs out of his aunt's hair as they walked briskly back down the pavement.

"*That* is Garfield Garsnipe!" said Aunt Thea, wrinkling her nose with disgust. "A revolting man! He has been bullying everyone around here into selling their houses to him."

"But why?" asked Jack, and Aunt Thea paused and looked sadly from one end of the row of cottages to the other. Jack now realized that more than half of them were empty. "Because," said Aunt Thea, "through a very unkind chance, he owns the freehold of the land."

"But you own your cottage, don't you?" Jack peered at her, confused.

"Yes, I do Jack – but the *land* is what's known as leasehold. That means, although I own my cottage, I don't actually own the land it stands on – or my back garden."

"That's stupid!" exclaimed Jack. He and Lewis had been coming to Aunt Thea's cottage and

garden for as long as he could remember and he couldn't believe it wasn't really *hers*.

"Yes it is stupid. It's a very old law and it doesn't make sense any more, but nobody has changed it. And that means, in about a week, my garden won't really be my garden."

"But that's terrible!" gasped Jack. "That can't be right!"

"It's not right," agreed his aunt. "Everyone kept trying to buy our gardens from Mr Garsnipe and he kept refusing, because he knew the time of the lease was nearly up, and then he'd be able to make our lives very difficult until we gave up and sold our houses to him – very cheaply – and let him do want he wants with his land."

"And what does he want to do?" asked Jack, fearfully.

"Bulldoze everything and build a great big load of flats," said Aunt Thea. "Lots of people will want to live here by the river. He'll make a lot of money."

"But – but – doesn't he need special permission from the council for that?" asked Jack, flabbergasted.

"Yes – and he's as good as got it. The town needs more housing. We poor cottagers don't really stand a chance."

91

"So . . . the standing stone," Jack whispered. "Will he really knock it down?" He couldn't imagine being able to play Tauronia games without the standing stone. The Taurs would just fade away without it.

Aunt Thea gritted her teeth as they stepped back up her path to the front door. "He'll have to go through *me*!" she said. "I'll chain myself to it if necessary!"

Jack looked at her in awe and realized that she meant every word.

Chapter Eleven

Stuff and Nonsense

When they got into the house, Lewis was no longer in the kitchen, but there was a faint smell of mead wafting from it, and they could see his drawing of Slashermite, damp and wobbly on the table. They had a quick look at it and saw that the tail was now complete, with a rather handsome green curl on the end of it. Aunt Thea washed her hands and face and shook her hair thoroughly over the kitchen sink, and then they went back into the garden.

Slashermite was running round and round in circles on the lawn, giggling and gurgling with delight. His new bit of tail had grown already and he looked like a mad sheepdog, trying to catch it. Jack gave a shout of laughter and caught hold of the small monster. "Let me see!" he said, and Slashermite jiggled up and down, pulling his tail

93

up and waving the handsome green curl under Jack's nose. He was beaming.

"Good job, Lew!" said Jack. Lewis was sitting next to Electrotaur at the foot of the standing stone, and grinned back. "It worked really fast!" he said. "It only took about two minutes to grow!"

"What about the new power, Lewis?" asked Aunt Thea. "Did you remember that?"

"Of *course*!" said Lewis, scornfully.

"Well?" said Jack, impatiently. "What did you give him?"

"I can—" squeaked Slashermite, but Lewis said "No! Let him guess."

Jack peered at Slashermite and ventured, "Um . . .

he can breathe fire? No . . . too much fire stuff, already. OK – he can fly!" Lewis shook his head and Jack went on, "He can spit out brand-new sweets whenever we want them!"

Lewis grinned again. "Nope!"

"Um . . . he can climb walls, like Spiderman? He can speak in any language? He can do all your homework for you, magically – and always right – in about ten seconds!"

Lewis cackled. "No. You'll never guess!"

"Well, tell us, then, Lewis," said Aunt Thea, sitting down on the other side of Electrotaur, who was still humming contentedly.

Lewis leaned in towards them, his blue eyes sparkling. "He can hypnotize!" he breathed. "Really and truly! He can totally hypnotize people!"

Aunt Thea sat up straight and peered at Slashermite. She looked slightly concerned.

"Anyone?" she said.

"Anyone!" said Lewis. "But *only* when I tell him to! He can't do it on it his own."

Aunt Thea breathed a sigh of relief.

"I should do mine, now!" said Jack. "I have to sort out Electrotaur's stupid trousers and give him a new power too, or it's not fair!"

"I'm afraid it's going to have to wait until

tomorrow now," sighed Aunt Thea. "I promised your mum you'd be back by three o'clock and it's half past two now. Come to me tomorrow tea time and you can sort Electrotaur out then."

Jack was disappointed. He couldn't believe he had to wait until after school tomorrow – after everything that had happened that weekend.

"Cheer up, Jack," said Aunt Thea, ruffling his hair. "Your Taurs will be safe with me. Nobody can see them here – not that there are many people left to see into my garden anyway," she added, with a sad smile.

On the way home, Jack told Lewis about what had gone on in the garden of the empty cottage, and about the terrible thing that could happen to the standing stone. Lewis was shocked silent. He didn't say anything for the rest of the walk home, but now and then Jack could hear him humming quietly.

When they got home, Mum was waiting for them in their bedroom. She looked grave.

"I'm wondering, Lewis," she said, "how you can explain this?" She opened her fist and a small shower of duvet stuffing fluttered down on to the carpet. Jack bent immediately to pick the bits up, while Lewis stared at Mum, his mind whirring desperately.

"I can't believe what you did!" said his mum, and pointed at his unrolled duvet – the nasty mess inside it and the ribbons of blue quilt cover created by Slashermite's finger-blades. Lewis bit his lip and wondered what to say. Just then, Scrag the cat wandered in and sat on the carpet. Lewis felt bad, but he had no choice.

"It was Scrag," he said, mournfully. "But it was my fault."

"Scrag?" said Mum, staring at the poor innocent cat.

"Yes – I was hiding inside the duvet cover and pretending my fingers were a mouse and Scrag was chasing it. I didn't realize he was scratching right through it. I'm really sorry."

Jack looked from Lewis to Scrag and felt guilty too.

"Sorry, Mum," he said. "We should have told you this morning. I helped Lewis clear it up – then we . . . we forgot to tell you." Jack felt bad about joining in with the fib, but what else could he do? Mum wouldn't ever believe the truth – and if they took her over to meet Electrotaur and Slashermite she would probably faint first and then phone the emergency services as soon as she woke up.

"Well, I'm not impressed at all," murmured Mum, looking at them both in turn.

They looked at their feet, feeling bad, even though they knew it wasn't their fault.

"You will both do without pocket money for the next three weeks," said Mum. "And *you*," she gave Scrag a poke with her toe. "Out!" The poor cat gave her hurt look and slunk away, miffed.

Mum shoved the mess of bedding into a couple of bin bags while they watched, forlornly. "Tea in an hour," she said, as she went out of their room. "Play quietly until then please. We'll get some spare blankets for you later, Lewis."

The door closed behind her and Jack and Lewis let out shaky sighs, before sinking down on to the carpet.

"We'll have to do something about that," said Jack, pointing to the Lego box, which was hiding more slash marks. Lewis nodded. He looked around the room and spotted an old rug, with a network of roads, traffic lights and buildings printed on it. When they were younger they used to play with their cars on it. They hadn't used it for ages and now it was squashed down behind the dressing-up

box. Lewis got it while Jack shifted the Lego box and they spread it out neatly across the slash marks. It looked fine and if they kept it fairly tidy, Mum would probably leave it there. They got out some cars and played quietly with them on the rug, remembering that it was fun and silly and nothing to do with monsters and standing stones and digging machines that tore up lovely gardens.

Chapter Twelve

The Hum Dial

Toroneeyans! Toroneeyans!
Its time to do yor quest now!
Come heer the thing we lowdly sing
And try to do yor best now
The time has come to do the task
That Jack and Lewis kinedly ask
Toroneeyans! Toroneeyans!
Plees anser ar reekwest now!

Jack looked up from the bit of paper covered in Lewis's uneven handwriting and stared at his little brother in amazement. The spellings were dodgy, as Lewis had trouble with reading and writing, but Jack could work it out. "You made this all up? By yourself?" he asked.

Lewis skipped a little along the kerb, smiling, and nodded. He had done it during the lunch

100

break at school. "It's the Tauronian Battle Song. We have to learn it," he said. "We can't just read it. That'll look really pants. We have to be able to sing it when the time comes."

"What's the tune? Have you made one up?"

Lewis shook his head.

"This is a tune you already know," he said. "You remember *Oh Christmas Tree?*"

Jack nodded and sang, "*Oh Christmas Tree, Oh Christmas Tree – how fresh and green your branches.*"

"That's it," said Lewis. "Well – the words fit that exactly. Try it." Jack sang the Tauronian Battle Song in the same tune and Lewis was right – he had made it fit exactly.

Jack chortled. "So, have you thought up a quest, too?"

Lewis shook his head. "Me neither," said Jack. "We're a bit pants too, aren't we?"

"They're going to get fed up with us soon, if we don't," said Lewis. "Quests about sitting in holes or bushes, or doing a bit of gardening . . . well, they're not very *Tauronia*, are they?"

They arrived at Aunt Thea's by four o'clock, still practising the song, and found a note on the door. It read: *Jack & Lewis. Tibbles.*

They grinned. It would make no sense to

anyone else, but they knew exactly what it meant. Tibbles was the name they had given to a large, smooth white stone that Aunt Thea had somehow brought back from Scotland. It was about the size and shape of a small dog, curled up as if asleep. Jack had called it Tibbles years ago and a couple of times, during treasure hunts at Aunt Thea's, they had found things hidden under Tibbles.

Jack dug his fingers quickly under Tibbles and unearthed a pale blue envelope. In it was the front door key and a note: *Hello you two. Our guests are downstairs, having a rest. I have had to go in to town to argue with the council. Please let yourselves in and take our guests into the garden if they want to go. I will be back before you know it. Love A T*

They unlocked the front door and looked around for signs of the Taurs. "Downstairs," said Jack. "I think she meant the cellar. She wouldn't risk leaving Slashermite anywhere near her Persian rugs." They opened the door under the stairs and called, "Hello, Slashermite! Hi, Electrotaur!" Slashermite immediately scampered halfway up the steps to meet them. Electrotaur just buzzed up from below. In the cellar it was bright and warm and dry. Central heating pipes ran all around it, keeping it quite comfortable,

102

and they saw that Aunt Thea had laid out some cushions and blankets across the stone floor, as well as some plastic beakers – one with a little apple juice still left in it and one with several squashed batteries clumped inside. Two plastic plates had sugary bits on them. It looked like both Taurs had been enjoying some more doughnuts.

But now Electrotaur was standing up and all around him were small glittering discs. Lewis squinted at them and realized they were perfectly flattened drinks cans. Slashermite picked one up and plopped it into a wicker basket with a dry rattle of aluminium.

"What on earth are you—?" began Jack. "Oh, hang on – let me guess. A quest?"

"Yes," said Slashermite. "We must defeat the evil Lord Landfill."

"Well, good. That's a great quest," said Lewis, a little too eagerly. Electrotaur gave him a sarcastic look and stamped hard on a cola can.

"Have you been down here long?" asked Jack.

"Half of the clock!" said Slashermite, eagerly, and they saw that Aunt Thea had put a large, round alarm clock on a shelf.

"Has Aunt Thea been teaching you to tell the time?" laughed Jack.

"She said that the young creators would come when half the clock was gone," said Slashermite and Jack realized she must have left at half past three, just as they were getting changed out of their school clothes and setting off from home. The big hand had moved half an hour, and here they were.

"C'mon," said Lewis. "Let's go up and play in the garden 'til she gets back."

"PLAY," said Electrotaur from the corner, abandoning his stamping. "WHAT IS PLAY?"

"It's . . . having fun," said Jack. "It's how we – er – enjoy ourselves."

"ENJOY?" said Electrotaur.

"Just . . . do things we like. Because they're nice."

"NICE?"

"Oh, for goodness sake, Electrotaur. Follow us!"

Out in the garden it was peaceful and pleasant. Jack found it hard to believe that it didn't really belong to Aunt Thea. The garden and the standing stone were as much a part of her as her brilliant red hair and her strange clothes. Slashermite and Lewis started chasing each other around the lawn, giggling and squeaking. "Blades *in*, OK?" Jack shouted, worried. Slashermite, though, already had them tucked away. He was getting quite good at being

careful. There had been no slash marks in the cushions or blankets in the cellar.

Electrotaur walked stiffly past them all, glowing gently against the greenery and emitting the occasional blue spark. He made for the standing stone, and once more, sat down at its base. He looked very relaxed there. Jack sat down next to him, feeling the hair on his right arm prickle up with the static around Electrotaur.

"Are you OK, Leccy?" he asked, trying to sound like a mate.

"I AM WELL," said Electrotaur, not moving at all.

"So . . . you don't . . . thirst? Or hunger?"

"I AM WELL," repeated his creation.

"Nothing you need, then?" persisted Jack.

"I NEED ONLY THE QUEST."

"Oh – that. Right. Well, it's on its way." Lewis and Slashermite were trying to do forward rolls now, which was a bit unfair on Slashermite, because the rhino horn on his forehead kept sticking into the lawn. Jack sighed and wished again that he had thought up a monster that he could play with too. Electrotaur was cool, but you couldn't really even touch him much. You would always be worried about getting a shock. It was a shame – because he'd be fantastic for piggyback

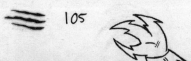

rides. You could see for miles up on Electrotaur's back.

Suddenly Jack remembered the main reason they'd come back today. It was so he could do *his* extra bit of drawing and spill the last of the Merrion's Mead! Maybe he could sort out Electrotaur right now! Jack ran into the kitchen and found their drawings neatly piled with the crayons and the twiggy bottles, still on Aunt Thea's table. He sat down, pulled his picture out and quickly got a red crayon. In the middle of Electrotaur's golden chest he carefully drew a red circle, and around this he put several small marks, spaced apart evenly. With a purple crayon he added a deep purple button right in the middle of the red

circle, and around the lower part of the red circle, outside it, he marked a curved line, with an arrow on one end.

Pleased, he sat back and smiled. Then he picked up his twiggy bottle, shook the watery mead inside it, uncorked the top and carefully poured the magic liquid across the picture. He waited a few minutes, gazing at the picture and concentrating, and then ran out of the kitchen and down the garden. Electrotaur was exactly where he had been before, but he had changed. In the centre of his chest was a round red dial, with a glowing purple light in the centre. Little lines marked even spaces around the dial, and there was a curved purple arrow around the bottom half.

"What is it?" panted Lewis, who'd just chased him down the garden. Slashermite panted too, exactly in time with Lewis.

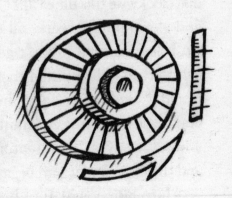

"It's a sort of volume dial!" grinned Jack, delighted. "It's there so we can turn

107

Electrotaur up or down. Make him a bit safer – or a bit more dangerous. Watch!"

He leaned forward and turned the dial anticlockwise and as he did so the occasional sparks stopped coming off the end of Electrotaur's tail, and the intense blue glow in his eyes faded. His hum went so quiet they could only just hear it.

"You OK, Leccy?" asked Jack.

"I AM WELL," said Electrotaur in exactly the same voice – only quieter. Jack touched his golden arm and felt no static at all. His own arm was normal, with no hairs trying to rise up. Slightly nervously, he touched his fingers to the cheek of the dragon-like head. Electrotaur's eyes blinked slowly but he was calm and still.

"OK. . ." said Jack. "Now watch." He turned the dial clockwise this time. "It's OK," he said, as the hum and glow and the sparks all came back. "The dial itself is insulated. I can't get a shock off it – even if I do this!" He whirled the dial around as far as it would go and Electrotaur's hum became *really* loud, and sparks shot in a constant stream off his tail and around his eyes. The creature was vibrating visibly and the grass under him began to crackle and steam.

"Turn him down! Turn him down!" yelled Lewis, looking very alarmed.

Jack beamed and paused before doing the best bit. He pointed his finger into the middle of the dial on the rumbling chest and then gave it a sudden jab on its glowing purple button. Immediately

there was silence. Electrotaur's head slumped forward and the fierce glow in his eyes shrank to two tiny green dots in wells of black. "Emergency cut-out button!" said Jack, chortling. Lewis gaped. "It's all right," said Jack. "He's just on standby . . . like the telly. Watch." He prodded the purple button again, and Electrotaur immediately raised his head and continued to hum and glow as he had done before.

"It's a reset button, too," explained Jack. "It puts him right back in the middle of the dial, where he should be. You OK, Electrotaur?"

"I AM WELL," said the Taur. They all laughed in relief.

It was brilliant. Really brilliant. Right up to the point when the wall fell on them.

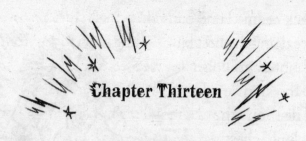
A Sing Song

It didn't even crash or thunder, and later Jack realized that the noises which should have warned them had been drowned out by Electrotaur humming and buzzing.

The old red brick wall crumbled over with a crackle of torn ivy and a series of dull thuds and clunks.

Slashermite let out a squeal and Lewis yelled in pain as chunks of wall struck them both on the shoulder and back and legs. Jack got a nasty blow on his ankle and hand and Electrotaur bellowed metallically as another brick struck his scaly toe. There was a moment's silence as pink brick dust rose high in the afternoon air and then Jack yelled, "Lewis! Lewis! Are you OK?"

"Ow, ow, *ow!*" said Lewis and Jack scrambled across to where his little brother was pulling bricks

off his legs, revealing some nasty grazes on his knees. Slashermite squeaked and Jack saw that his knobbly purple ankle was streaked with green blood.

Then Jack heard a familiar rumble and looked up in astonishment to see the *digger*! The digger from yesterday had just shoved down Aunt Thea's wall, and now it was moving along down the other side of the remaining wall, and turning to shove the next bit over. Jack yelled, "HEY!" and leaped to his feet, his painful ankle forgotten. He jumped across the remains of the wall and tore down the next door garden to the digger and its driver.

Garsnipe Junior was listening to a personal stereo and singing along with it in a loud, tuneless voice. He was turning the digger round and lifting the big shovel for another bash and wailing, "*And I kno-ooow that my heart will go o-ow-ow-on. . .*" when Jack threw himself into the cab for the second time and yanked him out by his head.

Just like yesterday, he let out a shriek and then bawled, "Not *you* again! Gerroffme! Gerroff!"

He rolled about while Jack pulled his little headphones off and shouted, "You pea-brained idiot! You nearly killed my brother! You nearly killed my brother!" Garsnipe Junior gaped at him and

111

then sat up, shoving him over on to the grass.

"What are you talkin' about, you little squirt?" he mumbled, getting to his feet.

"How *dare* you bash over my aunt's wall?" yelled Jack. He was just about to launch himself again at the digger driver when two strong hands grabbed hold of his wrists.

"What is going on?" growled a voice that he immediately recognized as Mr Garsnipe's. Jack wrenched himself around and stared furiously at the man, who still had the egg-spattered tie and grubby suit on and smelled of cabbage.

"Your idiot son just pushed a wall over on us, that's what!"

Mr Garsnipe glanced up the garden and saw the mess. "Anyone die?" he asked, mildly.

"No – no thanks to you! We could've died though – if it had hit our heads."

"Well, in that case," said Mr Garsnipe, with a mean grin. "You'd better make sure you get out of the way while the rest of the wall goes down."

Jack was staggered. "You *can't do this!* It's my aunt's garden!"

"Oh no it's not, son," said Mr Garsnipe. He pulled a folded bit of paper from his pocket and opened it up. It had town council lettering at the

top and looked very official. "As of today, all the land along this road belongs only to me – and there's not a thing you or your aunt can do about it. Now if madam *wants* to carry on living there, surrounded by a building site, and then a concrete car park, maybe I can't stop her. But I don't think she'll like it much." He gestured to his son, who had now crawled back into the digger, shooting Jack dark looks. "Get on  with it, Bill. I'll take care of the runny-nosed kids." He grabbed Jack's shoulder and propelled him back up the garden, over the fallen bricks and back into Aunt Thea's side. Jack looked around wildly. He could see no sign of Lewis, Slashermite or Electrotaur – but striding up the garden in a billowing red silk coat and black boots, and *steaming* with rage, was Aunt Thea.

Garfield Garsnipe saw her and let Jack go,

putting his hands on his hips and smiling meanly at her. "Time's up, Miss Casterbridge!" he said. "If you still want to sell to me your cottage I might consider it . . . but my offer's dropped to half the price now."

"Not on your life, you smelly little man," said Aunt Thea. She took hold of Jack and checked him over quickly.

"It's just my ankle," muttered Jack, still prickling with fury and longing to thump the man by the wall. "Where's Lewis?"

Aunt Thea glanced back at the cottage and said, "He's inside, drawing."

"*Drawing?*" said Jack. "At a time like *this?*"

There was a rumble as the digger turned itself around and began to move back towards the gap where the wall had been and suddenly Jack gave a shout of horror as he realized what was happening. Aunt Thea, too, began yelling. "Oh no! No you *don't!*" and she sprinted up the garden, her scarlet silk coat tearing out behind her like a flag, and threw herself against the standing stone.

"Give it up, woman!" shouted Garfield Garsnipe. "It's just a big pebble. Go and see Stonehenge!"

Aunt Thea backed up against the stone and glared at him, and then another part of the wall fell

114

over, sending bricks bouncing at her feet. "If I get one bruise from this, I'll have you arrested," she yelled. Jack skidded to her side and placed himself against the stone, too, but Aunt Thea shook her head and said, in a low voice, "Jack, I can't have you here. I would never forgive myself if you got hurt. Please go back into the house and hurry Lewis along!"

"But I'm not leaving you here!" gasped Jack, as the digger shoved the lower part of the wall down and began to roll its caterpillar tyres across the bricks towards them. "I'm going to protect the standing stone!"

"Jack," insisted his aunt, giving him an urgent look. "The best way to help is to go and *hurry Lewis up*!"

Jack realized that something else was happening. He hurtled down the lawn and into the kitchen. There he found Lewis alone, holding up a dripping piece of paper. "What is it?" he asked, panting.

"No time to tell you," said Lewis, blowing on the wet drawing. "Quick – can you remember the song?"

"The *song*?"

"Yes! The Tauronian Battle Song! You said you'd learn it! We need it *now*!" And Lewis put the paper on the draining board, seized Jack's arm and hauled him back out into the garden.

The digger was right over the border now, its

115

grimy yellow teeth against one side of the stone. Jack cried out as he heard the terrible grinding noise of metal against rock. He could see that Garsnipe Junior wasn't really hitting the stone hard; he didn't dare. He was just trying to scare Aunt Thea away so he could really shove it over.

"OK, Jack! NOW!"

Jack stared at Lewis in amazement as his brother began to sing, loudly and proudly, to the tune of *Oh Christmas Tree*, the Tauronian Battle Song:

"*Tauronians! Tauronians! It's time to do your quest now!*"

Shakily, Jack joined in, and then their voices were both loud and proud.

"*Come hear the thing we loudly sing, and try to do your best now*

The time has come to do the task, that Jack and Lewis kindly ask

Tauronians! Tauronians! Please answer our request now!"

Jack felt the hairs rise up on his arms, his legs, up the back of his body. The air suddenly felt electric, as if a tremendous storm was hovering above them. He looked at Lewis and saw his brother's teeth were chattering and his hair was standing up like a dandelion clock again.

Suddenly a warm rush of wind swept across the garden. Aunt Thea's hair blew out like a fan and Jack realized it was coming from around the standing stone. The digger engine started to whine and clatter and Aunt Thea suddenly stared down the garden at them, her eyes glittering with excitement. "Oh, well done, Lewis!" she said. "Well *done!*"

"Again!" shouted Lewis. "Louder!" And once more they launched into the Tauronian Battle song.

"Tauronians! Tauronians! It's time to do your quest now!"

Jack didn't know *what* was going on, but he knew something amazing was about to happen. The warm wind was circling the garden now. His own hair was standing up like Lewis's and the council letter that Garfield Garsnipe still held in his yellowy hand was flipping about like an angry snake. Both men were looking at each other uneasily, but the digger engine clattered and whined on.

"Come hear this thing we loudly sing, and try to do your best now!" Jack and Lewis were grinning at each other now, singing louder and louder. There was a rumble beneath them.

"The time has come to do the task, that Jack and Lewis kindly ask. . ."

A deep crack appeared in the grass under Aunt

 117

Thea's feet and she gave a whoop of delight and skipped off to one side.

"*Tauronians! Tauronians! Please answer our request now!*"

There was a brilliant flash – brighter than any lightning Jack or Lewis had ever seen and suddenly ribbons of glowing blue light were racing up and down the standing stone like a helter-skelter. The grass around it began to steam and the crack widened.

"What? What?! Whaaaa...?" shrieked Bill Garsnipe. He began to grapple desperately with his controls, trying to back the digger away from the glowing, crackling lightning ribbons that were still chasing madly around the stone. He was too late though, because one of the ribbons paused and suddenly poked out into the air like a curious finger. It jabbed once in the direction of the yellow metal beast and then leaped across to skip along each of the muddy yellow teeth on the shovel. A second later, the whole of the digger was covered in racing ribbons of electrical storm.

Garfield Garsnipe stood with his council letter still writhing madly in his fist, gaping at the stone. Aunt Thea was cackling with laughter and looking slightly like a stylish, red, mad witch, thought Jack. Just when he thought the scene couldn't get any

more amazing, there was a deep, deep rumble, and the standing stone began to *rise up*! Slowly and steadily, the base of the red and black rock emerged above ground with soil and roots and a few surprised looking worms and woodlice on it. It rose higher and higher, towering into the air until it was double the height it had been, and all the while the electrical ribbons tore around it and buzzed and whined like small fireworks.

"Dad! Dad!" wailed Bill Garsnipe, bouncing up and down like a toddler who badly needs the toilet, inside the digger. His dad ignored him. His eyes bulged.

There was a click and a grating noise and suddenly a door opened in the stone. Amid the blazing purple rectangle that shone out from it, stood the mighty form of Electrotaur.

Chapter Fourteen

EEEEP!

Electrotaur walked grandly out of the door and Jack felt a swell of pride. He looked magnificent. He was burning blue and sparking fabulously. He walked like a warrior across the lawn towards Garfield Garsnipe. The man shrank against the rough corner of the half-demolished wall and held his hands up in front of his face, dropping the council letter, which whipped away in a small whirlwind. Electrotaur stood in front of him and then tipped his amazing dragon's head down to look, his eyes shining a green torchlight across the man's screwed-up face.

For a moment he just hummed and stared and then he opened his mouth and said, "YOU TRESPASS."

Mr Garsnipe squawked. "I – I – I . . . it's my land. . ." he whined.

120

Electrotaur repeated himself, slightly louder. "YOU TRESPASS."

Mr Garsnipe peered up at the monster from under one of his elbows. "But . . . but I *own* it," he wheedled, miserably.

"NO MAN MAY OWN THE STANDING STONE OF TAURONIA. IT IS SACRED," explained Electrotaur.

"If you like," said Aunt Thea, "Electotaur will take you inside, so you can *see* that it's sacred. Or do you still think it's just a pebble?" She was hugely enjoying herself.

"No, no, no – no, I c-can see w-what you mean now, M-Miss Casterbridge," replied Mr Garsnipe, still hiding under his arm as best he could. "P-perhaps we should talk about this another time."

"Oh, I don't think so," said Aunt Thea. "I think *this* is exactly the right time. Would you like to meet our other friend?" There was a scratching noise amid all the humming and buzzing and Slashermite scrambled through the rock doorway, his toe-blades grinding daintily on its stone step. He scampered across the garden and jiggled up and down in front of Garfield Garsnipe, who was so astonished that he sank to his knees, where he was able to look this new monster right in the eye. Slashermite stared back at him and suddenly lifted his hands and slid all his gleaming finger-blades out fully, as if he were opening a fan. Mr Garsnipe whimpered.

"OK, Lewis, please ask Slashermite to do his thing," said Aunt Thea. For a moment, Jack thought she meant to get Slashermite slashing – which seemed a bit extreme even for nasty, smelly Garsnipe, but that was not what she meant. Lewis was now whispering in Slashermite's purple ear. Slashermite nodded and then he began to curl his finger-blades in and out in a wave. In and out, in and out, one after the other, from left to right, as if he was practising on an invisible piano. It was fascinating to watch – hypnotic – and now Jack realized what was happening and he chuckled with delight. Garfield Garsnipe dropped his arms and sat back on his heels. His mouth fell open and his eyes went dreamy, following Slashermite's fingers from left to right and right to left.

"You are getting very sleeeeepy," said Slashermite and Garfield Garsnipe nodded and dribbled a little bit. "Verrrrrry sleeeeepy," added Slashermite. Lewis whispered in his ear and he went on. "Do you hear everything I say?" Garfield Garsnipe nodded. "Good. Then hear what you must do." He nodded again. Lewis whispered some more and Slashermite continued. "You will find all the people who you bullied into selling their

houses, and you will sell the houses – *and* the gardens – back to them. For half the price you paid." Mr Garsnipe nodded and Lewis whispered some more. Slashermite pressed on. "You will rebuild the walls, sort out the gardens – and then you will go home and rethink your life." Jack was *sure* that bit came from *Star Wars*.

Lewis whispered again and Slashermite said, "You will apologize to Aunt Thea for being rude to her, you will send a large hamper of cakes and sweets for Aunt Thea, Jack and Lewis. And. . ." Slashermite paused as Lewis giggled into his ear and added his last instruction. "Whenever anyone says *fish* you will stand on one leg and go *Eeeep!*"

"Lewis!" scolded Aunt Thea but she was laughing. "That's naughty. At least . . . make it a less common word."

Lewis burbled something at his monster and Slashermite said, "No – not fish – but pterodactyl."

"Pterodactyl," said Lewis and immediately Mr Garsnipe got up, stood on one leg and went "Eeeep". They all fell about laughing. Mr Garsnipe just put his foot back on the ground and stared at Slashermite, still hypnotized.

"Anything else we should make him do?" asked Jack and they were just trying to think when there was a sudden clank and rumble behind them and they realized they had forgotten someone. And they'd realized too late. While they'd been talking, the electrical helter-skelter around the standing stone had settled down to a soft blue light and a gentle buzz, releasing the yellow digger – and its driver.

Bill Garsnipe had obviously got a grip of himself – and now he had a grip of the digger controls too. He was laughing and shouting at them all. "Who's the boss now, eh? Who's the boss now?" He trundled across and lifted the big toothy shovel high up above Electrotaur's head.

Aunt Thea yelled, "No! Stop it, you idiot!" Jack knew it was too late. The digger shovel was already sailing down and it struck Electrotaur's head so hard there was a ghastly metallic clang and sparks flew in every direction.

 124

"How'd you like that, eh? How'd you like that?" Bill lifted the digger arm up again, getting ready to go for another blow while Electrotaur swayed and then turned unsteadily around to glare at his attacker. Bill looked scared and fumbled as he got the arm up again. He was right to be scared. Electrotaur's dial suddenly shot up to full power, of its own accord. Jack gasped – he didn't remember dreaming up *that* bit, but he guessed it must have been in the back of his mind when he'd done the drawing. Electrotaur was like a walking firework now, sparking in all directions, rumbling with power and charging up the air again. During Slashermite's hypnotism session they had barely noticed that their hair had settled down – but now it was prickling up again and that hot smell was all around them as Electrotaur took a step towards the digger.

Suddenly, Jack realized how dangerous this was. Bill was now so terrified that he'd abandoned the controls and was sliding sideways out of the cab. This was a mistake. The cage of metal around him, set upon its rubber tyre tracks, had kept him safe from electric shock while the standing stone was growing and opening up. Now he had no protection at all as he stumbled on to the floor and cringed before Electrotaur. The giant blue monster advanced steadily and steam rose from the grass around each footstep. "NO!" shouted Jack. "You idiot! You've made him mean! Run! RUN!"

But Bill couldn't run. He wallowed about in the bricks and dirt, his little eyes bulging with fright. Electrotaur bent stiffly over and put out two buzzing golden hands. Fine crackles of lightning shot out of his fingers towards Bill and Jack knew he had to stop it. He ran across and around Electrotaur and shouted, "STOP! Stop, Electrotaur!" But Electrotaur didn't seem to be able to hear. Perhaps because there was a nasty dent in his head.

The electricity was now so strong around him, Jack could feel his skin twitching. If he didn't do something, he and Bill would both be cooked. Jack took a deep breath, tried to keep his hand steady and, swinging it right through a small tongue of lightning from his creation's outstretched fingers, he jabbed into the centre of Electrotaur's chest and hit the purple button. He was immediately thrown backwards so fast that the garden around him blurred, like the view from a train window. He hit the wall on the other side of next door's garden with a sickening whump. Then everything went quiet.

As Jack blearily tried to get his eyes working he made out Lewis coming towards him, his face white. "You OK, Jack?" he said, kneeling down in front of his brother. Jack shifted his arms and legs carefully, and they moved quite normally. He sat up straight and knew he was going to have a big bruise on his shoulder blades tomorrow – but he seemed to be OK.

"I think I am," he said. "What about *him*?"

"Oh, *he's* all right," said Lewis. "Keeps making noises like a sheep though."

Bill was, indeed, going "Ba-ba-ba-ba-ba" while Aunt Thea sat him up and made sure he wasn't injured. "Don't be such a baby," she said. "You didn't get shocked at all!"

Electrotaur stood motionless, still leaning over with his hands outstretched. Garfield Garsnipe was

127

exactly as they'd left him. Still hypnotized. Aunt Thea said it would probably be a good idea to hypnotize Bill too, or he'd go on bleating all day. Slashermite started his finger-blades thing again and soon got Bill calm and sleepy, like his dad.

"Now," said Aunt Thea, hugging Jack and Lewis fiercely, "I think it's time we finished all this. For a start, let's send these pathetic men home. I've looked at their nasty faces quite enough for one day."

Lewis led Slashermite into position in front of both men and said, "OK, tell them that when they wake up they will be very calm, and they will remember all their instructions. They will sort everything out as they have been told. And they'll be very kind to people from now on. Then count backwards from five and wake them up."

Slashermite did exactly as Lewis had asked and a minute later Garfield Garsnipe and his son were standing in front of them, smiling. "Good heavens, that was quite an adventure," beamed Garfield. "I thought I might wet my pants at one point." The boys fell into peals of laughter.

"Me too," said Bill, mildly. "And then I did."

Aunt Thea beamed back at them. "Yes, it certainly was an adventure. What do you think of my standing stone now?"

"I think it's quite amazing," said Garfield.

"So, have you remembered your promise?" asked Aunt Thea.

"Absolutely, Miss Casterbridge," said Garfield. "I will sell the houses and gardens back to everyone at half price and I will make good all the damage and I will send you and your nephews a hamper of cakes and sweets and I will go home and rethink my life."

"And I'll do as he says," chimed in Bill, eagerly.

"When do you want me to start?" asked Garfield.

"Tomorrow will be quite soon enough," said Aunt Thea. "I think you should go home now and make your wife some tea."

"Righto!" said Garfield, and he hopped back over the broken wall, with his son trotting after him.

"Pterodactyl!" shouted Lewis and Garfield Garsnipe stopped, stood on one leg and went "Eeeep!" before continuing across the garden and down the passage.

129

Chapter Fifteen

Tauronia

There was a grating noise and a sucking wind pulled across the garden. They all looked around and saw that the door in the standing stone had closed and the pillar of rock was sliding steadily back down into the earth. Within a few seconds the noise had stopped, the stone was still and a few birds began cheeping nervously in the trees again. Apart from the broken wall and some scorch marks on the grass, you would never have known what had happened in Aunt Thea's garden.

Slashermite folded his finger-blades away and stood quietly next to Lewis. Jack stared at his little brother. "Did you really draw all that?!" he breathed.

Lewis nodded but looked shocked. "I drew some of it . . . but it was *much* better than I drew!"

Jack walked over to Electrotaur and peered at

him anxiously. The tiny green dots were there, but even though Jack knew he was just on standby, he felt a pang of worry. There was a great big dent across Electrotaur's brow. What if he was damaged? What if he didn't come back on again? Nervously, Jack stretched out his arm and prodded the purple button. There was a click. Then silence. Jack's heart pounded. Then there was another click and a whirring noise. Suddenly the hum surged back, the green light flooded out of Electrotaur's eyes and the creature stood up straight, dropping his arms.

"Electrotaur!" shouted Jack, in relief. "You're back! Are you OK?"

"I AM WELL," said Electrotaur. He turned and headed straight for the stone. Then he sat down again, with his back against it.

"You're not hungry? Thirsty? Haven't got a headache?" questioned Jack, who had followed after him like an anxious mother. He knelt down and touched the dent on Electrotaur's forehead. His creation didn't seem to mind.

"I AM WELL," he repeated. "I DO NOT THIRST OR HUNGER. HERE, I AM WELL."

"Of *course*!" said Aunt Thea. "Why didn't I think of that? It's obvious!"

"What?" said Lewis.

"The standing stone! Of course – it's a power supply, don't you see? Like a great big battery. It's full of phenomenal cosmic power! That's why Electrotaur hasn't been thirsting – or even hungering! He's charging himself up with the serpentine rock!"

"I AM WELL," said Electrotaur again. "DID WE COMPLETE OUR QUEST?"

"Yes!" said Jack. "You did brilliantly! Sorry I had to turn you off for a bit, but you were about to electrocute someone, and that's not allowed."

"OUR QUEST IS DONE," said Electrotaur, and Jack saw that he was looking at Slashermite, who was nodding slowly back at him. "WE NOW MUST GO."

Jack was stunned. He'd forgotten about the end of the quest. Only two days ago he and Lewis were desperate to get rid of their monsters, but now. . .

"Where will you go *to*?" asked Lewis, quietly.

Electrotaur moved his head around and looked at Lewis. "I DO NOT UNDERSTAND."

"He means, where will you be? After today?" said Jack.

Electrotaur looked blank. Slashermite answered. "Nowhere. We will un-be, as we were before," he said, and he sounded sad.

"No!" wailed Lewis, suddenly hugging Slashermite. "I don't want you to un-be! You can't un-be! It's not fair! Stay with us."

"Oh, Lewis," sighed Aunt Thea, touching his shoulders. "You must see that it would be very hard for Slashermite and Electrotaur to stay. They don't really belong to our world. They can't hide in my cellar for ever, and if they just wandered off, sooner or later something bad would happen. Don't you see?"

"No – I *don't* see!" said Lewis, crying. "It's not fair!"

Slashermite looked at Lewis and then at his feet. Jack thought he might be crying too.

"Wait!" he said. "Don't go yet. Just wait a bit. . . We need to. . ."

Aunt Thea looked at them all gravely. "Can you both wait here while we go and talk in the kitchen?" she asked Slashermite and Electrotaur. They nodded and Slashermite sat down next to Electrotaur.

"Don't you dare un-be!" Lewis called back urgently, as Jack led him back down the garden.

In the kitchen Aunt Thea pushed fresh paper and crayons across to them. "I think," she said, "that it's time you both drew Tauronia."

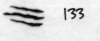

"Tauronia?" echoed Lewis.

"Yes – that's where all your Tauronian monsters live, isn't it? I expect it's a lovely place and even if there are baddies there, the goodies always win."

Jack and Lewis grinned and started drawing. "There's always lots of lovely food and drink," Jack said. "And Electrotaur and Slashermite have the best castle to live in, by a waterfall."

"Or how about a volcano?" asked Lewis, his eyes shining.

"No – too hot for them. That's a Lavataur place."

"OK, a castle, then, and they can go under the waterfall and down into the lake with Aquamite

sometimes," agreed Lewis. "And they can have ant porridge and doughnuts whenever they want them."

The pictures grew more colourful and detailed, but it didn't really matter how much they squeezed on to their paper. The dreams in their heads went on and on, and that was the main thing. In a few minutes they both held up their pictures, but then Jack looked stricken.

"It's no good!" he said. "It's no good at all! We've used up all the mead!"

"No, I think we have a little left," said Aunt Thea, picking up both bottles and shaking them.

Incredibly, there did seem to be a little more – even after Lewis had dropped some on his last picture.

"Quick, then!" said Lewis. "Let's spill it!"

"OK – I think you only *need* a few drops, you know," said Aunt Thea. She shook a bottle hard over each picture and a few drops spattered across them. They waited a minute, and then could wait no longer. They all charged back up the garden to Electrotaur and Slashermite.

"You're not going to un-be! You're not!" yelled Lewis, joyfully.

The creatures stood up uncertainly.

"Listen!" said Jack. "Your quest is done, yes, but what we didn't tell you is that you get a reward. You never go back to not being. You go to Tauronia – it's a fantastic place, which is your home. There are loads of other Taurs there. Some are good and some are bad, but you're good and you always win in the end. You'll have lots of quests to do for yourself."

"And you live in a castle by a waterfall and eat all the ant porridge and doughnuts you want," said Lewis.

"Look around the back of the standing stone," urged Jack, excitedly. "Look!"

They all trooped around the stone and on the other side, three feet up from the ground, was a

little nobbly bit of stone, standing out like a button. "Press it!" said Jack. Electrotaur did, and at once another rectangle of light shone out. This time it was golden light. At the foot of the doorway, smooth stone steps led down into the earth and curved out of sight.

"THIS GOES TO TAURONIA?" asked Electrotaur and Jack nodded, delighted. The doorway was his idea.
"THEN, GOODBYE, CREATOR," said Electrotaur and he bowed stiffly at Jack. He then bowed even more stiffly to fit inside the door, and walked away down the steps, his blue glow shining up through the golden light and then getting dimmer and dimmer.

"Goodbye, Electrotaur," called Jack, in a strangled voice.

Slashermite hugged Lewis, with his finger-blades carefully tucked away and Lewis hugged him back. "Bye, Slashy," he mumbled and then Slashermite scampered down the stairs after Electrotaur. They heard his toe-blades scratching on the stone as he wound down and down the spiral stairwell, and then there was a sound like a zip being done up fast, and the doorway filled with golden light simply vanished. In an instant the smooth red black rock with its nobbly button was all that was left. Jack pressed it again, but nothing happened. He realized that they'd only dreamed of Electrotaur and Slashermite opening it up. No human being would ever be able to follow.

They were all very quiet as they went back into the house. Aunt Thea made hot chocolate and they all sat together on her big squashy settee and drank it in silence.

Eventually Jack spoke, forlornly. "We'll never see them again, will we?"

Lewis sniffed. "I really glad they went to Tauronia," he mumbled. "It's brilliant in Tauronia. But I'm really going to miss them."

"We should have dreamed that we could go down there, too," said Jack, miserably. "Now everything's back to normal and it'll never be the same again. If only we hadn't used up all the mead. Now it's all over."

"Good grief, what a pair of mopers you are!" said Aunt Thea. She got up and walked across to the kitchen and opened her tallest cupboard. "Want some biscuits?" she said in a muffled voice.

"No thanks," said Jack and Lewis, sadly.

"Want some cake?"

"No."

"Want a bottle of magic mead?"

Jack and Lewis looked at each other. Aunt Thea pulled her head out of the cupboard and gave them a curious smile. At once, Jack jumped to his feet and ran across to her. Lewis followed.

Aunt Thea shut the cupboard door and leaned back on it. "I'm not sure you should look in here," she said. "It might be dangerous."

"*Aunty!*" urged Jack. She moved aside and they threw back the door. Up on the very highest shelf, standing in a neat row, were *six* twiggy bottles of Merrion's Mead.

"You got *more!*" gasped Jack. "Why didn't you tell us?"

"It only arrived this afternoon," said his aunt. "As soon as I woke up this morning I phoned up the shopkeeper who sold it to me to find out if he had any more – and then I paid a shocking amount of money to have a Welsh taxi driver bring all of them down for me. He got them here in four hours. I have to confess, I topped *your* bottles up just a little before I went out this afternoon."

Jack felt an enormous beam stretching his face.

He'd never been so delighted. "So we *can* go and see Slashermite and Electrotaur! We can!"

"No," said Aunt Thea, firmly. "I don't think you'll be able to go Tauronia. It's probably not quite real enough to be safe. But we can definitely have Slashermite and Electrotaur up to visit from time to time – *if* you promise me that we always do it together! If you can't promise me that, I'll tip all the Merrion's Mead down the sink."

"Yes! Yes! Of course we promise!" squeaked Jack and Lewis.

"When can we start?" gasped Jack. "For one thing, I've still got to sort out Electrotaur's trousers!"

"Give me a chance!" said his aunt, shutting the cupboard and sitting back down at the table. "I need to get over all this adventure first. So do you! And then there's your schoolwork to think about – to say nothing of the safety of mankind to consider! We can't just pop a monster out of the lawn every other day, you know."

"No?" Jack and Lewis did their best cute smiles and big eyes.

Aunt Thea sighed. "Well . . . how about Wednesday?"